SEX & SEDUCTION

A collection of twenty erotic stories

Edited by Cathryn Cooper

Published by Accent Press Ltd – 2007
ISBN 1905170785 / 9781905170784

Printed and bound in the UK by
Creative Design and Print

Cover Design by
Red Dot Design

Contents

Coming Soon	Elizabeth Cage	1
King Dong	Landon Dixon	9
The First Deadly Sin	Gwen Masters	17
The Tie Breaker	Phoebe Grafton	29
Library Rendezvous	N. Vasco	41
Mother Knows Best	Landon Dixon	53
Changing Objectives	Jeremy Edwards	67
Don't Quote Me	Lynne Jamneck	77
I Say His Name Out Loud	Adrie Santos	83
Choices	Kate Franklin	89
Flash Flood	Lynn Lake	103
Well Suited	Jordana Winters	115
Bananaz	Dee Dawning	123
Crazy Has A Name	Gwen Masters	139
Murder, Whores And Money	Teresa Joseph	145
Getting Waxed	Jade Taylor	155
Night Of The Bear	Garrett Calcaterra	165
Personal Enquiries	J. Carron	183
Test Drive	Roxanne Sinclair	195
Much Ado (About Nothing)	Sue Williams	205

Coming Soon
by Elizabeth Cage

I checked my watch for the seventh time in as many minutes. Face it, Mel, I told myself, he isn't going to show.

I was hovering in the foyer of the local multiplex cinema, in my short skirt, denim halter-neck top and strappy high heel fuck-me sandals, looking like a woman who had been stood up by her date. Which I was.

I flipped open my mobile, telling myself that maybe I hadn't heard it ring when he called to leave a message for me, which he must have done, if he'd had to cancel. If some kind of emergency had occurred. But there were no messages.

I'd met Bill at a Pilates class. He was the only guy in a group of ten women, so he kind of stuck out, so to speak. I was impressed that he was brave enough to join an all-female class – and by his physique. He had a really toned body and I liked watching his muscles when we did the press-ups, imagining that I was spread out on the exercise mat beneath him as he lowered himself down on strong arms and then, with a grunt, pushed back up.

I decided to chat him up after the class, we went for a drink, hit it off and then went back to his place for a great sex session.

Initially, it was passionate, steamy, animal fucking. He had tremendous stamina and I loved feeling his big hard cock pumping inside me. But he also liked to tease, thrusting, filling me, while I gripped with my (greatly improved from Pilates) pelvic muscles, and then he would raise himself up, taking all his weight off me and slowly, carefully, pull out of my slippery, aching pussy until just the glistening tip of his wonderful cock was barely touching my wet gash.

He'd stay like that until I begged him to fill me again, my arms and legs wrapping around his waist, his back, desperate to be fucked. It was torture, but exquisite torture, and he would bring me to a point where I couldn't stop myself coming, repeatedly, at which point he gave me a huge, smug grin before shooting his load with a cry like an injured wolf.

I felt smug, too, at landing such a great lover, ignoring several of my mates' warnings that he had a bit of a reputation as a user.

'Hey, he can use me all he likes,' I responded, remembering those great orgasms.

We'd been out twice since then – once to a club, another time to a wine bar. I didn't know if it was going to go anywhere, but the sex was so good I really didn't care: as long as I got my fix.

Bill only came to a few of the Pilates classes, said he never really stuck at anything; just liked to sample different things. I should have realized that included people.

I glanced at the crowds filing past me to the box office. It was Saturday night and this was a popular movie. And, of course, just to rub salt into the wound, the audience was mostly couples

The film was due to start in five minutes. I had a choice. I could go home, feeling sorry for myself, and get drunk. Or call a friend, and get drunk. Then again, I could always go in and see the film on my own.

It wasn't something I'd ever done before. I imagined I'd feel self-conscious, like when you're in a restaurant eating alone. In which case, I always took a prop, like a book or my laptop. I'd picked up the cinema's free Coming Attractions magazine but I'd read that twice just waiting for Bill.

Why was I so hung up about seeing a film alone? God, I was a grown-up woman. I'd suggested we come to the cinema because I really wanted to see this film. I'd been looking forward to it (and the sex which would have followed). Of course, I could always wait until it came out on DVD, I supposed. Relieve my frustration with my favourite vibrator.

I watched as the last of the queue dwindled and people disappeared into Screen 1, the really huge screen with Dolby surround sound. It would have been fun. Damn it, I wanted to see whether Uma did get to kill Bill. I almost laughed at the irony. Because right now, I felt like killing him myself. And the idea of seeing Uma kick male ass really appealed.

'One, please,' I said, thrusting a ten pound note at the bored-looking teenager in the box office. Probably doing a weekend job while he was finishing his A-levels at school.

'We only have a few seats left. Where do you want to sit?'

I wanted to sneak in and sit at the back, unnoticed. When I was sixteen, you could sit where you liked in the cinema and preferably at the back with your mates so you could mess about, and have a snog and a fumble. I hated having to choose my preferred position from a computer screen.

'What about in the middle of this row?' he suggested.

The lights had already gone down when another teenager with a uniform shone a torch at row F and I had to ask people to get up, as I stumbled and pushed against them. I felt like they were all staring at me, and a few muttered, irritated that I'd left it so late. I kept whispering 'Sorry' until, finally, I got to my seat.

I glanced either side of me. I was between a girl snuggled up to her boyfriend, her tousled blonde head resting blissfully on his shoulder, and a guy in a light coloured shirt and dark jeans.

Trying not to fidget unduly and further annoy those who were already comfortably settled, I sat down and discreetly adjusted my skirt. There wasn't a lot of room for manoeuvre here, because I'd chosen to wear a very short, flimsy little number that barely covered my thighs. Okay, so it wasn't entirely my choice. Bill had suggested I wear something that would enable him to 'get at me easily' in the cinema. At the time, I was more than happy with this idea but now I frowned, deciding to send him a nasty little text after the show to tell him what I thought of him. However, to hide my immodesty, I left the film magazine on my knees to cover some of the exposed flesh.

I was still fuming about Bill as twenty minutes worth of advertising was bombarded into the cinema, which simply added to my irritation. Finally, the main feature began and I focussed on the screen.

The film was at the bit where our poor heroine has been buried alive in a coffin, with seemingly no way of escape when I felt something brushing against my ankle. I ignored it at first hoping the cinema didn't have a rodent

4

problem, but as it continued I peered down to see that the guy sitting next to me had moved his leg across so the leather of his shoe was touching my bare ankle. I froze.

He was staring intently at the screen, as if he hadn't noticed. Perhaps he hadn't. Maybe he didn't realize we had made physical contact. I carefully shifted my foot away and decided to ignore it. My focus returned to the screen, and nothing further occurred. I was relieved that I hadn't ended up sitting next to some pervert, particularly in the mood I was in. But, after a while, I felt the slightest of pressure against my calf, so slight as to be almost imperceptible, which made me doubt the sensation.

My eyes dropped down and I saw that his leg was touching mine, the roughness of the fabric of his jeans creating an interesting sensation against my bare flesh. Hmmmm. I wondered what to do next. By rights, of course, I should give him a sharp kick at the very least, or stamp on his foot with my lethal stiletto heel. Then he'd get the message. But while I was deciding, I allowed myself to savour the sensation a little longer, which wasn't exactly unpleasant. Quite the opposite, in fact. So when I felt fingertips trailing gently across my thighs, I wasn't surprised.

Perhaps he'd interpreted my inaction as unspoken consent to what was taking place. And what exactly was taking place? An erotic exploration of sorts in a large darkened room full of other people. I was in no danger. I was quite safe. And I knew somehow that if I indicated to him to stop he would immediately do so. I wondered if anyone else could see what he was doing. Somehow that heightened the excitement, because I was, despite myself, getting a bit of a thrill from this.

His touch was incredibly light and gentle, as if he was stroking the most precious velvet, sending little tremors through me.

Although I could see the screen, hear the brilliant soundtrack, the great music, the witty dialogue, I was also in a parallel universe which consisted of pure physical sensation.

As his fingers moved, he could sense my arousal and perfectly judged when and how to step up the action.

I trembled as his hand moved slowly, inexorably, up my thighs and under the hem of my flimsy skirt. Then he stopped, as if unsure of whether it was safe to proceed. I was torn between indignation, outrage and excitement. But I was turned on. Big time!

I breathed deeply, audibly and he moved his hand further and higher, until I could feel the tips of his fingers caressing the insides of my thighs; my pussy lips, already moist, tantalisingly close.

He found the thin fabric of my lacy thong, pushed it to one side and then I thought I heard him gasp softly as he realized I was shaved, completely.

I froze like a rabbit caught in the headlights of a rapidly approaching car, mesmerized.

Then his intrepid digit found my opening, slipping inside while his thumb stroked my clitoris.

I stared ahead, unable to bring myself to look at him. Normally, I would have been groaning loudly by now but having to stay quiet, to pretend that I was fully engrossed in the film, heightened the excitement, the illicitness, the sheer naughtiness of what he was doing. It was our secret.

But it was hard to deny my vocal chords release, and I realized with exquisite horror that if he continued to minister to my wet pussy in this manner, I would almost certainly come. And almost as soon as I'd allowed the thought expression, I did come. Suddenly, blissfully. And silently. I thought I was going to pass out, as the waves racked my body, drowning me. For a moment, I closed my eyes.

When I opened them again, wondering if I had dreamt what had just happened, I let my hand rest on his, and he turned over my palm, his grip gentle but firm, moving my hand away from my own body and placing it carefully on his lap. I was shocked to feel his unsheathed cock, hard as a rock, and took a sideways glance.

He had folded his jacket and laid it across his groin, unzipped himself (had he been wanking himself with his other hand while he was making me come?) and my hand was beneath it, resting on his rod.

So while I lusted after David Carradine on the screen, savouring his amazing sexual charisma, I brought off the stranger in the seat next to me. It took a matter of seconds and it made me feel powerful, like Uma.

When the film ended, I wasn't sure whether I should get out quickly. He might be embarrassed. I didn't know what to expect. Except I knew I was curious. I was also feeling randy again. Then the lights went up and it was my first chance to look at him properly and he at me.

He smiled uncertainly and I smiled back.

'Do you want to go somewhere?' he asked in a deep, smoky voice.

I nodded. 'Yes.'

Together, we walked through the crowds into the foyer.

'I know a place very close by,' he said, taking my hand. Walking down a corridor he whispered, 'Wait here.'

He disappeared into the men's toilets, where I imagined he would be using the condom machine.

Minutes later, he reappeared, grabbed my wrist and pulled me into one of the cubicles. I opened my mouth to protest, but he whispered, 'Shhhhhhh. I don't know about you, but I don't think I can wait until we get back to my place.'

Pushing me against the partitioned wall, he knelt down between my legs, lifted my skirt, ripped off my soaking wet thong and started to tongue me. I quickly experienced my second quiet but incredibly powerful orgasm of the evening.

While I was still reeling, my legs shaking, he rammed his rigid cock into my waiting, very open pussy. My pelvic muscles instinctively gripped him like a vice, milking him until he exploded inside me, at which point we both placed a hand over the other's mouth as we came, desperate not to be discovered.

We heard several guys come in and go out during the next few minutes and when the coast was clear, we crept back into the corridor like a couple of naughty teenagers.

Outside the cinema, I decided to introduce myself. 'I'm Mel.'

He grinned sheepishly. 'Steve. Thanks for a lovely evening, Mel.'

'It's not over yet,' I pointed out.

'Very true. You know what I want to do right now?'

I shook my head, deciding that nothing would surprise me about this guy.

'This.' And he opened his mouth and screamed. Loudly, as if he was coming all over again. I quickly joined in, vocalising the ecstasy I'd experienced during the past couple of hours but had been unable to give vent to.

'That feels better,' he sighed. 'What now?'

I took his hand. 'Back to my place for some good, old-fashioned sex. In a bed. With no noise restrictions.'

'Sounds good to me. By the way, what did you think of the film?'

King Dong
by Landon Dixon

I gunned it through the iron gates, up a blacktop lane that looped its way to the barn-sized front door of the Bisbey mansion. I slid out of my jalopy and stared at the architectural monstrosity – two glowering storeys of red brick and bronze gargoyles, fronted by Southern gothic pillars that put rotted teeth into the ugly face of the building. For the middle of the Great Depression, it was quite the joint. The discovery of oil in the LA basin had enriched a chosen few, when most were shuffling their tired dogs through bread lines and unemployment offices.

I eschewed the ornamental brass knocker and hammered on the door with my fist. A servant led me into the hushed, cool confines of a marble-carpeted hallway, up a winding staircase clothed in red velvet, to the second-floor study of the mistress of the manor.

Her name was Etta Bisbey, and she was seated behind an oak-panelled desk large enough to float twenty Titanic survivors. She rose, sashayed around the varnished expanse of wood, giving me a good gander at all she had. And, baby, she had plenty. Her large, round breasts strained the buttons on her pearl-white blouse like Fatty Arbuckle's claims of innocence strained credibility. The rest of her wasn't soup kitchen fare, either: pretty face, pitch-black hair piled atop her gourd by the same skilled, effeminate artisans who weave gold out of dross, a slim waist, and shapely, slender calves and ankles peeking out from under a sapphire-coloured skirt.

I pumped her extended hand. 'You said on the phone you wanted me to find something,' I stated, talking shop while my eyes took inventory. I dangled my hat over my crotch, to conceal a rather rude case development down there.

'Yes, Mr Polk,' Mrs Bisbey responded. 'An item of mine – an objet d'art – has been stolen, and I must get it back.' Her hand fluttered about her throat, then down the side of her breast.

Her voice and mannerisms were a little too exaggerated for my taste; I smelled ham. 'You an actress?' I asked, impressing her with my whiskey-clotted powers of observation. What babe with a built-for-bed body like hers, living in sunny, sinny LA, the widow of an oil tycoon who, when living, had more wrinkles in his dick erect than flaccid, wasn't a current or former actress?

She pirouetted away from me, strutted to the window and gazed out at the Hollywood Hills, perhaps doing a visual size comparison. 'Why, yes, I was a thespian of some renown – at one time,' she remarked.

I studied the wicked silhouette of her generous tits and gave my pocket-rocket a surreptitious stroke of affection. 'What's been lifted?'

'I have a picture of the…item…in my bedroom.'

We adjourned to the room next door, a tastefully-appointed sleeping and sex flop big enough to shelter a Wobblies' convention. She pulled open a drawer in a walnut nightstand, took a picture out of the drawer, handed it to me. It was an 8 by 10 glossy of a black dildo –

a rather immense dildo if I was any judge of perspective, and pricks. I glanced from the picture to her, and her face went redder than post-war Russia.

'It's an object of no real value to others, but of great, uh, sentimental value to myself,' she breathed, twisting her hands. 'My father obtained it from a tribal chieftain in the Belgian Congo during one of his explorations many years back. It's supposed to bring its owner good luck.'

And great gushes of girl-goo, no doubt. I tossed the picture of the inflamed cunt-plunger on her bed, said, 'No dice, doll. I don't hunt sex toys – unless they're human.' I had a semi-reputable reputation to maintain, after all, and scurrying off on a clam digger expedition wasn't going to improve it any. I headed for the exit, stage-right.

'Mr Polk!' she gasped.

I spun around, and gaped in awe at her spectacular, naked upper body. 'Yiminy yaminy,' I murmured, ogling her twin, creamy-white globes, her jutting, pink nipples.

She cupped her huge, heavy tits and squeezed, her wrist strength incredible. 'Are you sure I can't convince you to handle my case?' she whispered.

I scratched the erect stubble on my chin. 'I guess if you put it that way,' I rationalized, tearing my hat and jacket off, ripping away my tie.

I grabbed her proffered jugs and kneaded the firm, warm, blue-veined flesh. Then I bent my head down, her tits up, and licked at her engorged nipples. I nursed on her rubbery nubs for a good, long while, then shoved her onto the bed and climbed aboard. I unhanded and un-mouthed her burlesque show boobies just long enough to fumble my pants and shorts down, her skirt open. I tore her panties apart and grabbed my cocked love-hammer and stuck it inside her pussy.

11

Then I froze like Scott at the South Pole. I was swimming down there! My sperm-shooter comes with a seven-inch barrel, fully-loaded, but it couldn't get even the slightest bit of traction in Mrs Bisbey's stretched-out man-catcher. I snorted, churned my hips, got absolutely nowhere. 'What are the actual dimensions of that missing dildo of yours?' I asked dejectedly.

'Well, it's about ten and three-quarter inches in circumference, I suppose, and approximately thirteen and a third inches in length. Its head is –'

'Stow it,' I groaned. 'I get the picture.' Obviously, her ebony plaything had spoiled her for any normal guy, ever again.

After making ourselves decent, Mrs Bisbey gave me the photo of her absconded art-piece/cunt-plug and strict instructions not to talk to her step-children, servants, or friends about the case. She claimed that none of them even knew about her thirteen-inch, blue-black dipstick, and that they could all be trusted anyway.

How the hell the busty broad expected me to get my mitts on a giant dong without chatting up any of her connections, I had no idea. But I agreed to follow her wishes – for the time being – and made my first pit stop Sol 'Gutsy' Gutzinger. Gutsy was a peeping-tom blackmailer who had kidnapped rich kid's pets for a living before he'd cleaned up his act. His shutterbug specialty was actors and actresses who could afford to pay to keep unwanted publicity private. He had a file and photos on every silver screen show-off from Zdeno Adams to Alma-May Zbitnew.

I slipped through the unhinged door that served as the entrance to the fleabag hotel he called home and office, took rotted stairs to the third floor, and strode into his dump, inadvertently scaring off an old geezer clutching a heavy-bound book like it was a stone tablet just come hot off the Mount. Gutsy also operated a pornographic lending library, when he wasn't making with the creeping ivy.

'What'd you got on Etta Bisbey?' I asked, tossing a crumpled twenty his way.

He was hunkered down on a ratty sofa, his fat mouth wrapped around a ham sandwich, his fat hand a bottle of beer. 'The film floozy that married the croaked oil baron?' he grunted, his porcine features gleaming sweat.

'Yeah, something like that. She lives out on –'

'I know where she spreads 'em, gumshoe,' he growled. He shoved more sandwich into his kisser, took a leisurely chug of beer, and waited.

I tossed another twenty into his crusty lap.

He set his snack down on the dust-coloured carpet, hefted himself off the tortured couch, and waddled over to a row of filing cabinets. 'Etta Vlat was the tomato's maiden name, if I 'member correct – which I always do.' He bent in half like a sagging tower of mashed potatoes, pulled out a drawer marked 'V', a file marked 'Vlat'.

He straightened up with a groan, thumbed through the file, then let out a wolf-whistle. 'Well, hello dolly! Kee-rist, I musta jerked off to this dame's films more'n any –'

'Spill the beans, Gutsy!' I barked, instantly regretting my choice of words.

According to Gutsy, Etta Vlat had been a stage and silent film actress in the late-teens and early-twenties – before my time. She'd been a real bankable cock-throb, until she'd had an affair with a black stagehand while still starring in a sham marriage with another matinee idol who was rumoured to stick his dick where the sun didn't shine.

13

The resulting scandalous abortion and divorce had deep-sixed her career quicker than leprosy.

The stagehand's name was Leonard Little and it was to his seedy address in Hollywood that I next directed my flivver. Ten minutes of phoning had confirmed his location in the city directory; he was the guy who too-vehemently denied ever knowing one Etta Vlat.

He rented number 306 in a grime-stuccoed building located next to an abandoned liquor store, and when I pressed my ear to his papier-mâché door, I heard the unmistakable grunting and groaning of the body-English language. I kicked the door open with a size-twelve and, snapping on the lights, beheld a black guy banging a white gal from behind, on a foldaway bed. The guy had a prosthetic penis rigged to his loins – a huge, night-shaded dong about ten and three-quarter inches in circumference and approximately thirteen and a third inches in length.

'What the fuck you want!?' the cock-strapped man yelled.

I pointed meaningfully at his dangling dick.

I sent Leonard Little's bed-buddy packing, then spoke to Little with my clenched fists for a minute or two, till he came bloody well clean. He and Etta had indeed been a pair back in the roaring 20s, until he'd knocked her up, flown the coop, and then tried to blackmail her and the studio by threatening to go to the papers. Etta had endured a near-death abortion experience, and she rewarded Little for his ungentlemanly behaviour by tracking him down and hacking his double-length dong off with a meat cleaver.

Time had passed, wounds had healed, and Little had resigned himself to a less-than-cocksure lifestyle, Etta to the well-paid role of career housewife. But then Little heard that Etta had turned a plaster cast of his prodigious prong, made in happier times, into a workable, rubberized dildo. Having his meat cleaved was one thing, but having his ex-lover pleasuring herself with his cock, while he wasn't attached to it, was too much. So, he'd taken back what he thought rightfully belonged to him – his manhood.

I relayed all of my juicy findings back to Etta, after she'd snatched the liquorice thunderstick out of my hand and started lovingly stroking it like a long-lost friend. When I was done with my monologue, she quickly paid me off, obviously anxious to get reacquainted with her black beauty. I headed for the study door as she raced into her bedroom, then I quickly backtracked and surveyed her from the crack in the bedroom door, to make sure I hadn't sold her a phoney bill of goods, of course.

She stripped out of her blue, tailor-made dress, her pink, silk under-thingies, until she was as breathtakingly naked as the truth, her bountiful breasts hanging huge from her rib cage. Then she bent down and yanked something out from under her bed. A blue-black corpse! No, upon closer examination, I saw that it was a life-size replica of the groin-gouged Leonard Little. I even recognized his outsize bellybutton. And as I stared in amazement at the black mannequin, Etta locked the colossal cock back into place with a deft twist of her wrist, and Little was big once more.

I slid my own rod out of my pants, rubbed it like the New Deal rubbed some folks the wrong way, as Etta hurriedly straddled her former lover's body-double, spread her puffy, pink pussy lips, and eased them over the mushroomed cock head of that towering pole, then down the incredible length of the snatch-shattering shaft. She groaned with unadulterated joy as the lethal cock-imitation sank into her sopping-wet puss like a lance into a Spanish bull, till the massive member was buried to the pre-formed balls in her glistening gash.

Impaled on that ebony-sheathed sword, she began churning her taut ass up and down, the dong sliding back and forth in her gripping, dripping sex hole, her breasts bouncing up and down with glee as she stuffed her warped pussy full of industrial-sized dick. I stared at her jouncing jugs, my hand a blur on my steel-hard cum-cannon, and when Etta cried out in blistering ecstasy, I saluted her spectacular show of nostalgic lust by coating her bedroom door and carpet with sticky, steaming adulation.

But the fun didn't end there. She quickly recovered from her long, hard pussy ride, reached back and spread apart her rounded butt cheeks, and split her anus in two on the dark, deadly dildo. I felt obliged to hold my post to the very end, and soon added even more substance to the gooey contents of the case file that I'd already emptied onto the floor.

The First Deadly Sin
by Gwen Masters

Adam and I had spent a wonderful, relaxing day together. Our vacations were few and far between, so we took advantage of every moment we could. We had driven all day, stopping at interesting places along the way, often pulling over to make love in a secluded grove of trees down some lonely side road. Now we were shopping for antiques in one of the quaintest little towns we had ever seen.

We parked the car at the end of a strip of antique shops and set out walking. We weren't looking to buy, only looking to look and to be with each other. Throughout the afternoon we browsed through old postcards and ceramics, played with antique wooden toys moulded by the hands of a hard-working farmer, and studied old quilts. Adam chuckled often at my enthusiasm. We didn't even notice as the sun began to hide behind dark storm clouds.

We were pulled out of our absorption with each other when a shopkeeper announced in a pleasant voice, 'I'm so sorry, but we're closing now.'

Adam and I held hands and hustled to the door, only to find that it was pouring rain outside. The storms had finally moved in.

'I hope I rolled up the windows,' Adam murmured, looking out at the rain.

'Too late now,' I said.

The shopkeeper allowed us to stay for a few minutes, but it quickly became apparent that the rain wasn't letting up anytime soon. In fact, the heavens seemed determined to drown everything beneath them.

I finally turned to Adam and smiled up at him. 'Wanna run through the rain?' I teased him. 'Just like we were kids again?'

Adam grinned down at me. 'We're not that old yet, are we?'

'You didn't seem that old last night.'

He laughed. 'Why not?'

We bid the shopkeeper a fond goodbye and raced out the door, holding hands and giggling like schoolchildren. We soon found that our plan had a little hitch; this wasn't a gentle rain. It was hard and punishing, the drops stinging like needles on our bare legs and arms. Our laughter soon disappeared and we huddled together under a tiny awning that didn't provide much protection.

That's when I looked up and saw the church.

St Joseph's Cathedral. Like all enormous Catholic churches, it was imposing and far too grand for the little town in which it resided. The soft glow through the stained glass indicated that we might find shelter there. The large rough bricks that built the façade were quickly darkening as they absorbed the moisture from the clouds. The door was huge, solid wood, and welcoming.

'Adam!' I yelled over the rush of the water flowing down the storm drains. 'The church!'

He didn't hesitate. We raced across the road and up the steep stairs, ducking our heads against the fury of the raindrops. He grabbed at one of the doors and pulled.

Nothing. The second door swung wide and easily on large hinges. Cool air flowed out of the church as we stepped into the vestibule and stood looking at each other. Water dripped from Adam's hair and down his nose, ran down his chin and dripped onto his chest. Puddles began to form under us.

Adam sighed and shook his head. 'Look at us,' he laughed, holding his arms out from his body. Water dripped off of him in constant little plops.

'At least we're dry in here,' I said. Adam reached for a choir robe that hung on a nearby hook, looking around to see that no one was watching.

'Shhhh…' he said to me as I took it from him and used it to dry off as best I could. Adam found another robe and used it to dry himself, then we hung them neatly back on their hooks. Somewhat presentable again, we walked from the vestibule into the outer chamber.

We stood in silence, awed by the power of the place. The ceilings were three stories high, and arched with solid oak beams. The ceiling was covered with a mural of the Virgin Mary, and the stained glass windows on either side rose two stories before joining the mural in a cacophony of color and priceless artistry. Even the pews were lovely, obviously hand-carved out of expensive woods. Three steps led to the massive altar. An imposing crucifix hung as the focal point in the massive church.

Adam, a sometimes devout Catholic, automatically dipped his fingers into the holy water at the back of the church and genuflected. He murmured something that was foreign to my Southern Baptist ears. His eyes were wide as he took in the church.

'It's beautiful, isn't it?' he whispered.

'Absolutely,' I agreed.

'Let's sit,' he prompted. The pew was surprisingly comfortable. Adam pulled his rosary out of his pocket and played with it, turning it over and over in his hands as I lay my damp head on his damp shoulder. We didn't speak; content to just look around for the longest time. I listened to his heartbeat and the silence.

'Is anyone in here, you think?' I asked him.

'I'm sure someone is nearby.'

I trailed my hand up and down his thigh. Adam quietly fingered the beads of his rosary while I stroked his leg. Maybe it was the heathen in me that my Baptist preacher never could quite talk away, but I found myself growing wet at the very thought of fucking Adam in a church. I don't know where the idea came from – maybe it was that polished table that boasted a long sentence in Latin, then below it: 'Do this in remembrance of me.'

'Adam?'

'Hmmmm?' He seemed to be almost asleep.

'I want you.'

'To do what?' he asked.

I snickered. 'No, silly. I *want* you.'

He looked down at me. I looked into his eyes, making sure he understood that I meant exactly what I said. 'I want you to fuck me in this church.'

Adam started to laugh. I didn't. He sobered very quickly.

'You are serious,' he stated flatly.

In response, I took the rosary from his hand and pressed it hard to his crotch. He grew hard almost immediately, despite the wide-eyed look of astonishment in his eyes. I moved the smooth beads around the outside of his shorts, then slid them up inside the leg of them to press them against his balls. Adam's hand covered mine to pull it away, and then he hesitated as I slid the beads up his hardening shaft.

I circled my hand around his cock and laced my fingers through the rosary. I slid both up his body and he exhaled the breath he had been holding, groaning softly into my neck as he opened his mouth and bit down. I gasped in pleasure as the wetness started to grow between my thighs.

'This is wrong,' he protested half-heartedly.

'Do you think so?'

I slid my hand up his shaft and pressed one rosary bead to the opening of his long cock. I pushed harder, gently pushing it in a little. Adam's hips jerked and his hand clamped down hard on my wrist, holding me there. I spun the little bead and he cried out, the sound muffled against my neck. I pushed the little bead in and out, in and out of that little slit on his head, fucking him with the cool hard pebble.

Suddenly Adam lurched up and yanked my hand away. He hauled me roughly into the aisle. He tried to push me to the carpeted floor and I resisted, pulling the rosary out of his pants and sidestepping him. My reflection looked back at me from the bowl of holy water. His eyes danced from me to the rosary as I reached in and dipped the beads into the liquid. Adam's mouth fell open in surprise. I walked to him and yanked down his shorts, suddenly exposing him to the angelic faces looking down from the ornate walls.

'What are you doing?' Adam hissed, his voice a frantic edge in the silence.

I was wrapping the rosary around his cock. He groaned aloud as I pulled it tight, circling it snugly around his hard tip, then rolling it down like a condom. Adam gasped as the beads rolled down to the base of his cock. 'I want you as hard as you can be,' I whispered, leaning forward to drink the drops of holy water that slid down his balls. Adam thrust upward toward my mouth and his hand found his cock. He began to stroke and I smiled mischievously.

'Isn't masturbation a sin?'

'You're a temptress,' he replied in his own defence. He squeezed his cock as I sucked one of his balls into my mouth. I ran my tongue over it and sucked, feeling it roll between my lips. Adam moaned quietly, the passionate sound resonating from the high ceilings and back down.

'Someone could walk in on us,' he protested.

'Someone probably will,' I responded. Adam's cock got even harder. I knew how he loved public places. I loved the sinfulness of sex in church.

'Would you like that, to have a priest walk in on you being fucked?' I taunted. In answer, his fingers found the rosary beads and pulled, making them tighter around him.

'Would you like to show a prim and proper nun what a real cock looks like?' I asked him. Adam stared down at me with eyes that were alight with desire.

'How about showing her what a real fuck looks like?'

I stood and wrapped my fingers around his cock, then gently pulled. Adam followed me obediently to the altar, and as I turned to him he sunk his hands into my hair.

'The altar?' he asked me, his voice filled with anticipation.

I sank down to my knees and opened my mouth over him, taking him down in one long stroke. Adam's soft cry echoed from the ceiling. I sucked him in until the rosary beads rolled against my mouth. Then I began to slide my mouth up and down, sucking his head, licking the first drops of salty moisture and sliding down to taste the last of the holy water between the rosary beads.

Finally I slid my mouth all the way down his cock, circling my lips around the rosary. I caught the beads with my teeth and slid them slowly up, caressing his cock with them as I pulled them off. He was bigger now than he had been when I put the beads on, and they were a bit difficult to remove. They squeezed tightly around his shaft.

I pulled them off and let them fall into my hand. My tongue flicked that spot right under his head. My teeth nibbled gently. I took the wet rosary beads and slid them down his balls, all the way back to his ass.

Adam tensed. I slid the beads up and down the cleft of his ass, letting the warm beads caress him, letting him get used to the idea. I sucked hard on his cock and then removed him from my mouth long enough to whisper to him.

'Relax…'

I pushed the rosary against him. I pressed one bead against his puckered ring. Adam whimpered and moaned on a deep breath as he let his body relax as much as he could. I gently pushed, and the bead disappeared, sucked into his ass as he clenched it against the feeling.

'Oh…oh, God…' Adam groaned.

He had completely forgotten about being quiet. I slid another bead to his tight hole and pushed. His body sucked it inside. I licked his cock with long strokes, sucking hard as I repeated the action with each bead on that rosary. Adam couldn't decide whether to buck his cock into my throat or push his ass against my hand. I kept it up until only the small cross on the circle of beads was left outside his body.

Adam looked down at me. His eyes were cloudy with pleasure.

'You…are…a heathen,' he murmured, breathing hard.

'You're Catholic,' I said. 'Which is worse?'

Adam offered me a quirky, sarcastic smile.

He lifted me to my feet and his hands found my shorts. He pulled hard. Seams ripped as he yanked them down my thighs and I kicked them off. I was wearing nothing underneath. Adam lifted me to the offering table, settling me on the cool polished wood. He climbed onto it. Bibles and a few candles fell to the floor with a thud. He pushed me up, then spread my legs wide and sank his cock into me with one fluid motion.

'Adam!' My voice was quiet, but still it bounced and echoed from the ceiling of the church. Adam thrust hard and deep. We were both on the edge already. Adam paused once, holding his cock deep inside me.

'Look,' he said.

I looked to where he nodded. He was looking at the magnificent crucifix on the wall.

'I'm going to tie you to that and make you come there,' he told me.

He began to pump in and out, harder and harder. I slid my hand down his back and found that cross that was lying against his ass. I came with a low, deep moan. I bit my lip to keep from crying out. I stared at the mural on the ceiling, watching the angels that hovered protectively above.

I circled my hand around the cross and began to pull. The beads slowly popped out of his tight hole, one at a time.

'Dear God!' he groaned.

He slammed hard into me, shoving me up the table, and I yanked hard on the beads. His cock throbbed inside me and he groaned again, this time with his hands buried deep in my hair. He kept coming as I slid the rosary out. Adam seemed to hold his breath for an eternity, and then he sucked in great breaths of air and collapsed on top of me.

'My God, My God,' he said over and over like a prayer.

24

Adam lifted me from the table and carried me to the front of the church. He stepped onto a platform that held the enormous crucifix. I had a sudden sharp moment of doubt. This was so wrong – wasn't it? All thoughts fled my mind when he lifted a long purple sash from the nearby pulpit and looped it over the arm of the cross, then around my wrist. He lifted another sash and did the same thing with the other arm. Then he unbuttoned my shirt and stepped back to look at me.

I was bound to the cross, my feet spread on the platform below me. The wood of the cross was rough against my back. Adam touched me with one finger as I looked out over the rows of pews. His finger slid down my body, circling each nipple before running down my stomach and over my curls. He paused to run the pad of his thumb over my hips before sliding his hand up again.

'Please, Adam,' I moaned.

'I'm thirsty,' he said softly.

My eyes flew to him. He looked calmly at me, stroking his cock with his hand.

'Will you feed me?' he asked.

Adam knelt between my thighs and spread them wider. His fingers touched my clit and I bucked up into him. The bonds around my wrists cut into me with a sweet, gentle pain. Adam quickly replaced his fingers with his tongue. He licked slowly at my clit then slid his mouth down to delve into my cunt.

'Give me my seed,' he murmured. 'Do it, love. Give it to me. I know you can.'

I tilted my head back. It thudded against the cross, and I saw stars. God, this felt so good! I squeezed my inner muscles, rhythmically, hard. Adam groaned in approval. The sound echoed through the church. Adam caught the moisture on his tongue. He licked and sucked and played until my knees were weak.

'I can taste us both,' he whispered.

I cried out as his tongue touched my clit and pressed hard. I squirmed before him. He licked hard and then sucked, alternating, keeping me on the edge.

'Come for me,' he whispered. 'Come for me in this church. Come for me on this crucifix. But while you do it, I want you to pray the rosary.'

'Oh, God!' I was right on the verge.

'Hail Mary…' he prompted.

'H…H…Hail…Mary, full of…grace…'

His lips closed around my clit. His teeth sank down, and I suddenly couldn't breathe. He bit down slowly, then harder, threatening me with the possibilities. I was riding a thin line between pain and pleasure.

Adam bit down harder.

I came viciously, my body convulsing on the cross, the pain overtaking me with pleasure. My hands clenched hard on the rough wooden arms, and the sharpness of a splinter sliced into my finger. My body throbbed. I moaned senselessly as my orgasm waned.

Adam kissed me as he gently loosened my bonds. I fell into his arms and he lifted me from the crucifix, carrying me down the stairs and the altar like I was a new bride.

'Where are we going?' I whispered. Adam glanced down at me and smiled.

'I know what I want, darling.'

He stopped in front of the altar and pulled out a small drawer under the remembrance table. I looked down as he settled me on my feet and I laughed at what he pulled out.

It was a communion cup.

'You have to be kidding,' I said.

He looked at me with the most serious expression he could muster.

'You need to take communion.'

I stared at him. He nodded. I sank to my knees before him.

My first long lick made Adam arch into my touch. The second made him groan. He hadn't come while he was licking me on the crucifix, and the sweet torture he inflicted on me had made him more than ready. I closed my lips around him and began to lick at the sensitive spot right underneath the head of his cock. I flicked my tongue across it. Then I gently sank my teeth into it.

He gasped and began to writhe under my ministrations. My hands found his balls and he almost laughed when he felt the cool beads of the rosary press against his soft skin. I circled the rosary around one of his balls and pulled gently, separating them, and my tongue circled around the other one before I gently sucked it into my mouth. Adam's whole body jerked and I tightened the rosary on his balls while my hand slid up to circle around him.

Holding his balls like that, I began to jack him off. Hard. I squeezed him with my hand as I slid up and let up on the pressure as I slid down. I slowly pushed him out of my mouth and looped the rosary around both his balls, clenching it tight. He cried out. I stroked him hard and flicked my tongue over his head before sucking him into my mouth again.

Oh, God…I need to come,' he moaned.

I pulled down harder on the rosary and he yelped. I slid my mouth down halfway and pulled on the rosary, the beads sliding and twirling around his balls. When I gave him a hard upward suck, Adam began to tremble. He cried out as he began to come.

I took the first shot into my mouth, then quickly squeezed his head hard. Adam moaned loudly in both pleasure and pain. I slid my mouth off him, licking gently, and released his balls. The pressure in his cock was enormous. I pressed the communion cup to the tip of his cock and let him go. His cock spurted out a few more times, filling the cup to the top.

'Wow,' he muttered, as he braced himself on my shoulder to keep from falling over.

I held up the communion cup and he grinned.

'Is this for me?' I asked him. He shook his head.

'For you?' I asked. Again, he shook his head.

'Get dressed,' was all he said.

I slowly dressed before him while he pulled up his shorts. We walked toward the back of the church. Adam took the communion cup from my hand. With a wicked smile, he stopped before the basin of holy water.

'No way!' I breathed in astonishment.

Adam winked at me. He tipped the cup and dumped his semen into the water. He swirled it around with one finger, then offered that finger to me to suck.

I was speechless. I watched the water drip from his fingertip and slowly moved toward it, as if in a trance. I licked the tainted, blessed water from his hand.

'Forgive me, Father, for I have sinned,' he intoned slowly, and that broke the spell. I laughed out loud. Adam opened the door and looked back at me with an expression of wry irony.

The rain had stopped.

'We're both going to Hell, you know that, don't you?' he asked me very seriously, and I couldn't help but laugh again. My voice echoed from the vaulted ceiling of the church.

The Tie Breaker
by Phoebe Grafton

To be fair, Gerald's a good tennis club chairman. He's able to devote a lot of spare time to it; possibly because nobody asks him to play. Not unless they are really stuck. Most times when they are that stuck they simply cancel the booking.

You see, from a tennis point of view Gerald's well past his sell-by date.

During Wimbledon fortnight I'm perched on the edge of my seat, hands sweating, body tensed, salivating over those virile, fast, macho hunks. As they sprint about the court with vigour and determination my squeals of delight are only interrupted by Gerald's gentle snoring in his chair in the corner.

Gerald used to be good…well reasonable. Credit where it's due.

He was runner-up in the inter-village play-off against Budleigh Salterton a few years ago.

Sadly there were insufficient funds available to provide a trophy for the runners-up, so the occasion went unnoticed.

Not that you can accuse me of being unsupportive. Didn't I take on the job as membership secretary?

It's a full-time job for it requires me to put the prospective club members through their paces.

It's not that I consider myself a better player, you understand. On the contrary, I have nothing to show for it. The trophy I won in the inter-village play-off against Budleigh Salterton vanished. Gerald claimed that it was taken by thieves after a break-in at the club house. Strange. Nothing else went missing.

New club members generally join in pairs as husband and wife arrive to settle in the village. There are occasions when an unencumbered male expresses interest in membership.

I'm then required to play them in a trial match. Some of the more, shall I say, active, new comers take a long time to recapture some sort of form. On such occasions trial sessions take simply ages.

In my defence can I submit that it has something to do with the very long winters we seem to get these days.

I'm not sure that Gerald trusts me absolutely. It all stems from that time Lorenzo was a club member. We don't get many Lorenzos staying in our village.

He was typically South American. Handsome, swarthy, charming, complete with smouldering brown eyes. Gerald hated him on sight. This was way back in Gerald's playing days.

My spouse swore that his dislike had nothing to do with the fact that Lorenzo used to leave him for dead each time they played.

Lorenzo and I eventually teamed up for mixed doubles. Then we both used to leave Gerald for dead in club matches. Poor Gerald, he was no match for Lorenzo.

This applied as much off court as it did when we played. From a woman's point of view the likes of Lorenzo pass through a girl's life only very rarely. To let one slip through your fingers condemns you to a legacy of lasting regret.

Therefore, to take the sort of drastic action necessary when an opportunity like Lorenzo presents itself, means that will-power just doesn't come into it at all. A girl's got to do what a girl's got to do.

So you see when Lorenzo and I went off to play an away match together, Gerald was not best pleased. He was much less pleased when we arrived back in the middle of the night.

The fact that I explained how Lorenzo's car broke down didn't cut any ice with the irate Gerald. Probably had something to do with the oily hand mark he later found on my bra. He didn't speak for days. All in the past, though, leaving Lorenzo, passionate Lorenzo, a wistful memory.

Early season brought an application from a Paula Spence. Gerald commented that her writing was atrocious. For all that he sent off the standard reply, with a trial game arranged for the following Saturday. The weather was indifferent which accounted for the fact that there were no other court bookings for that day.

It's a short walk to the club so ten minutes later I turned into the road leading to the courts when I was suddenly stopped dead in my tracks.

In the sort of double take that they do best on the movies, I took in the sleek Jaguar parked outside the clubhouse. What was standing beside it took my full attention.

My legs turned to jelly as he smiled in my direction. Had Roger Federer taken the wrong turning on his way to Queens?

I had trouble working my mouth. 'Good morning' came out like 'Gurr mooning'.

He smiled again, 'I hope this is the right place for the trial match?'

'I thought you were a woman. The application form said Paula.'

Stupid remark. You'd go miles before you saw anybody less like a woman.

'Sorry, my patients always moan about my writing. It's Paul actually'

We shook hands. His firm, strong hands and intensely deep blue eyes served to confirm my resolve. This was going to be a very long trial match indeed.

It was encouraging that he eyed me appreciatively when I took off my anorak. The short tennis skirt did my figure no harm at all. Neither did the tight tennis top which afforded a generous outline to complete, what I hoped, was an attractive figure. Time would tell.

We got into a knock-about almost immediately. It was obvious that Paul was match rusty. For all that the game was vigorous enough to ensure that we worked up a little sweat.

Only when we stopped after a quarter of an hour did I realize that even a sweat had its advantages.

As we went back to the clubhouse Paul couldn't keep his eyes off my heaving breasts.

Once inside the clubhouse the reason became apparent. A glance in the mirror showed that my exertions had caused the perspiration which had made the bra and the tennis shirt almost transparent. The nipples stood out hard and firm.

With drinks from the machine we sat lounging opposite each other exchanging small talk. As I sat with thighs slightly parted I had quite forgotten I was wearing a short skirt. Paul hadn't.

I felt his eyes like a caress. There was a long moment of silence.

'Are you a good sport?' he asked.

'Depends what you mean?'

'How would you feel about a little challenge? Like we play a game and say winner takes all?'

My mouth went dry. 'Takes all what?'

Even as I asked I knew the answer.

He smiled right through me. 'Winners choice of anything he…or she wants, OK?'

I tried to sound brave. 'Right,' I told him, 'you're on.'

So we played. To be honest he was still rusty. Yet for all that he managed to move about the court a lot faster than previously. For Paul there were too many unforced errors. It took me all my time to lose.

He looked boyishly pleased. He had conquered in two straight sets. By the time we got back to the clubhouse my shirt was sticking to me. It was a factor which did not go unnoticed by Paul.

We rested and had another drink from the machine. If it took a short while to cool down, I imagined it would take a lot longer to calm down. While I was sitting opposite Paul, outwardly composed, my body was demanding that he got on with it…and claim his reward.

He moved his chair closer. His hands rested lightly on my knee.

'I won,' he said simply.

'I know,' I answered thickly, voice full of anticipation, 'what must I do?'

He smiled into my eyes. 'Help me choose the prize.'

Even as he spoke his hands slid gently but unhurriedly towards my inner thigh. Paul was very forward for a doctor. I mean if he had intended to carry out that sort of examination he might at least have asked my permission

33

first. I would have given it readily, of course, but that's something else.

Such thoughts were fleeting as his practised hands slipped beneath the short skirt to meet at that place which was already tingling.

I had no intention of being a difficult patient. I lifted my bottom off the seat. My tight little tennis knickers offered little resistance.

He pulled them down, held them almost reverently for an instant, then tossed them carelessly over one shoulder. Bless him.

By this time I was beyond redemption. This was because his caring hands had resumed their exploration. With no barrier they soon discovered my prize.

I shuddered with unaccustomed desire as his sensitive fingers played wicked games.

Parting the lips he found the clit bidding a moist welcome to further ministrations.

I arched my body, moving forwards so that his probing fingers found an easy entrance. The impatience at our mutual discomfort was immediate as my body sent urgent signals for greater closeness.

When Paul stood up he looked decidedly uncomfortable. For a moment I thought he was carrying a spare racquet in his pocket.

I helped him disengage the trapped member.

When it sprang to view I realized the source of his discomfort. Proud and splendid. It certainly wasn't a spare racquet; nevertheless, it would take all of two hands to control it.

Our clothes provided stepping stones towards the old settee in the corner of the clubhouse. If progress towards it was slow at least it was a voyage of discovery. Paul learned the sensitivity of each nipple as they hardened in turn to the attention of his warm, but urgent, lips.

I, in turn, was fascinated by the thrusting insistence of his manhood as he pushed against me.

As I said Paul was big, hugely, wonderfully big and my body couldn't wait to devour his throbbing shaft.

The fire in my loins would only be doused by the coupling, that deep feeling of completeness which only maximum penetration would provide.

Pushing him down on the settee I pressed myself against him. The salt, sweaty, man smell of him fanned the further flames of my desire. I sent my lips on a journey, along the path which took the taste of him across the fur covered belly to rest against the hardness of his rampant cock.

Taking the sac beneath in both hands I gently massaged. Paul grunted his approval.

My tongue lightly ran the length of his twitching rod, as I licked my way around and up over its demanding head.

It was when I took the salty head in my mouth, moving my lips up and down, that I realized how near Paul was to completion.

If Paul ever entertained thoughts that this was to be his prize, then he was certainly not prepared for what happened next.

Standing astride him I lowered myself down upon his eager shaft. His eyes glazed. All resistance gone. I guided his stiff penis past the moist welcoming lips deep, so deep inside me.

Then I thrust my body down hard and immediately became totally impaled.

If Paul was momentarily stunned by my sexual mastery he soon recovered.

Grabbing my bottom he pulled my body down further upon his plunging tool. Shrieks of protest arose from the tortured frame of the old settee.

Three things happened simultaneously. Paul came, I came, and the settee went. The collapsing settee only served to ensure that Paul became more firmly embedded within me. Nice.

I felt his spurting cock pumping into the very centre of my being.

As an orgasm convulsed through me, my muscles contracted, milking his rod dry.

Finally he spoke. 'I thought it was supposed to be my prize?' he queried.

'Are you complaining?' I asked.

He gave me that boyish grin again. 'Not at all.' `

'OK, we'll compromise,' he said. 'Let's call it love-40.'

We lay in each other's arms amid the wreckage of the settee. Contented, I clung to him as he moved restlessly.

'Mind the splinters,' I told him.

Later he stirred again. 'Do you fancy another game?' he enquired.

'As long as it's not tennis.'

He reached for me. I lay beneath him, ready for more, bathing in the sea-blue eyes of this magnificent specimen of manhood.

With a kiss I motioned him to cease for a moment.

'Shall we find somewhere more comfortable?' I asked.

So we went hand in hand into the changing room. It's quite well fitted out with lockers, a massage bed overlaid with foam covering, as well as wash basins and toilets.

Paul led me to the massage bed and eased me down upon it.

Filling a wash basin he left me to return moments later with soap, towel and flannel.

Soaping the flannel he came to me. Parting my thighs he cleaned me, soaping me first then laying the flannel to one side.

His soft hands smoothed their soapy way across my lower body. Gentle, manipulative fingers teased once more around the lips of my responsive opening.

With the slightest hint of pressure his probing fingers massaged my clit until I lifted my body in supplication, my desire pleading with his fingers to become more adventurous.

He knew well of my need as he left me again, only to return seconds later to rinse and wash away the soap. Dabbing me dry he walked to the end of the massage bed and pulled me towards him.

When my legs hung useless and idle over the end of the bed he stood between my inviting thighs.

Paul had the sort of kisses that could set fire to any part of my body. To attempt to fire that part which was already a steaming cauldron of desire was to offer self control impossible odds.

My inner thighs moved with his lips, first as soft as butterfly's wings until they moved higher. Parting the lips of my vagina he curled his tongue to tease the inner flesh in clitoral stimulation.

I felt spasms of pleasure course through me. I reached down and pulled his head closer.

His tongue burrowed deeper into me as his sensitive mouth sought to extract completeness from my pulsing vagina.

Paul did not have long to wait. I wrapped my legs tightly about him, forcing him to stay inside me. I arched my body in that spasm of beautiful euphoric release which only a shuddering climax can bring.

I lay spent, but prepared, as he stood before me with his massive organ provocatively erect.

'Your prize.' I murmured.

'Let's call it deuce,' he said.

He stopped quite suddenly. I felt his whole body tense.

Looking again out of the window he said 'Who do you know that drives a green hatchback?'

I disentangled hurriedly. 'My husband.'

Paul may well have been rusty at tennis but he was dressed, with his hand on the door, while I was still scrabbling to get my clothes together. He stood for a moment at the door.

'How about my membership?' he asked.

'Guaranteed.' I told him.

'You won't be sorry,' he said with meaning.

That much I didn't need telling.

Paul opened the door and walked out along the path. He nodded to Gerald as he passed.

With seconds to spare I realized that I was complete. Except for my knickers. I found them where Paul had carelessly tossed them earlier.

Clutching them behind me I went out to meet Gerald. I fervently prayed that no capricious wind would lift my short skirt to reveal that tennis wasn't the only game we had played.

Gerald appeared not to notice my discomfort. He was too busy watching the sleek Jaguar easing its way down the road.

'Who was that?' my spouse enquired.

'His name is Paul Spence.'

'I thought he was supposed to be a woman?'

'Sorry,' I told him, 'I forgot to ask.'

'Funny… anyway what was he like?'

I clutched my knickers even tighter behind my back. A wicked breeze was blowing cool where no breeze had a right to blow.

'Not bad, a bit rusty but I'm sure his game will improve.'

'Any strong points?' he persisted.

'A good forehand.'

'How about his service?' Gerald asked.

'Ace,' I told him.

Library Rendezvous
by N. Vasco

'Can you believe it's been five years?' Anna said as her elegant fingers wrapped around Hector's broad, manly hand. She never stopped admiring his strong jaw and romantic, deep-set eyes.

'Feels like yesterday.' Hector replied while gazing into her smouldering, dark eyes reflecting the single candle on their table. His gazed wandered to her pouting lips and alabaster neck as he admired her tight yet beautifully curved body in the clingy black dress she wore that night. Her inviting cleavage and succulent breasts rose with each breath she took.

They occupied a booth in the corner of a fancy restaurant and were oblivious to the busy waiters and the chatter of diners. She placed a small parcel in front of him, her glistening, long red nails matching the color of the wrapping paper.

'Happy anniversary,' she said.

He loved her hands. She had recently taken to wearing a ring on each finger, adding to her already exotic look. Hector smiled when he unwrapped it, a book of erotic poems from the Sung dynasty. He raised her hand to his lips and gently kissed each finger.

41

She leaned close and whispered in his ear 'Look inside.'

He opened the book and saw a dainty, black thong panty hidden in the pages as Anna leaned even closer and covered his lips with hers. Her tongue probed his mouth in a quick, passionate manner as her dainty foot slipped out of her stiletto-heeled shoes and stroked his calf.

They parted. Hector sighed with pleasure and heard her giggle.

'What's so funny?' he asked.

'Yesterday I heard a woman say the first time isn't supposed to be…satisfying,' she replied.

It was his turn to laugh.

'Really,' she continued as the sensation of her dainty foot stroking his legs sent shivers up his spine. 'She said the first time is usually when two people don't really know each other. It's supposed to be an awkward moment.'

'Maybe for some people,' he replied while resting his hand on her thigh, the waist-high slit of her dress allowing him to feel the warmth of her skin through her black silk stockings. She snuggled even closer, pressing her breast against his chest as he gently squeezed that firm yet pliant thigh, her purring moans the only thing he could hear as he remembered the first time they met.

It was a rainy Sunday afternoon when Hector entered the campus library and saw Anna for the first time. He rarely went there on weekdays and preferred to do his research when there weren't as many students around to snicker at 'Doctor Love' behind his back. It was true he taught a course in human sexuality but he never failed to notice his classes were always packed when his lectures featured erotic Hindu sculptures or Japanese prints illustrating sexual techniques outlawed in some states.

42

He saw Anna sitting behind the reference desk, taking notes from a book, her glossy black hair set in a tight bun. Her high-necked, white, Victorian-style blouse and horn-rimmed glasses didn't take away from her dark, exotic features. As a matter of fact, her conservative outfit only seemed to complement her sex appeal and, before he could help it, Hector was fantasizing about enjoying her sensuous lips.

Suddenly, her dark, almond-shaped eyes fixed him for a millisecond before returning to her book.

She didn't seem to notice him at all.

'Might as well get to work,' he thought while finding an empty table in the reading area and taking out his notes. Minutes later he was distracted after hearing a chair move back and the 'tap' of high heels.

A lump formed in his throat when Anna walked past his table, her tight, grey, ankle-length skirt with buttons up the side hugged her sexy figure but it was her black, stiletto pumps that caused a rise in his pants he hadn't felt since he was eighteen.

'That's not library standard,' he thought, admiring the curve of her backside and the wonderful outline of a thong panty when she bent to get a book. She turned and headed back to her desk as he thumbed through the pages of his book and it wasn't until she reached his table he realized the book was a Chinese 'pillow book' filled with full page illustrations.

It was too late. He looked up in time to see her glance at it and raise her eyebrows as he threw her an embarrassed smile.

She walked away.

'Strike out for Dr Love,' he thought as she returned to her desk and picked up her phone. Not even the way she sat, one leg curled under her thigh, the gloss of her stiletto pumps reflecting the overhead lights, could distract him from his embarrassment. He got his things and snuck out the back door. Outside the rain was coming down in sheets. He realized he had left his umbrella on the table when some students shouted 'Taking a cold shower, Dr Love?' from a passing car.

Every day before going to work Anna always took time to admire her naked body in front of a full-length mirror and masturbate. She loved the way her luscious hips tapered from her tiny waste and the curve of her taught ivory buttocks. She pinched and scratched her rock hard nipples and cupped her high, up-turned breasts, the other hand stroking her naked stomach just above the subtle, dark patch between her legs as her eyes wandered down the long, supple length of her perfectly toned legs.

She decided to wear a pair of open-toed, stiletto heels and liked how the leather straps looked around her ankles, her thoughts still on the man she saw the day before. He had such a cute, embarrassed look on his face when he saw her looking at the very sexy illustrations in his book. Thoughts of joining him and looking at those hot pictures made her pulse race with excitement as her palm brushed the closely shaven hairs of her crotch just before her long, red-nailed fingers began to toy with her juicy pussy lips.

She had wanted to sit next to him but had to answer a patron's inquiry first. When she went back to say 'hi' his table was empty, except for the umbrella he had left behind.

'He'll eventually come back for it.'

She fantasized about being alone with him in the library and how turned on he would be as he watched her slowly unbutton her skirt, gradually revealing her toned legs encased in her black, silk stockings. By now, her other hand was cupping her buttocks. She always liked the way they curved out and the deep cleft between the twin hills of her juicy, tight cheeks.

The thoughts got even sexier. She now imagined him sitting on the chair, his pants around his ankles and his stiff, hard cock standing upright as she knelt between his thighs and masturbated while taking him inside her willing mouth.

'He probably tastes so nice,' she thought while brushing her nipples against the mirror, the cool surface making her gasp as she stroked away, her nails now digging into her cheeks. Suddenly, that familiar, erotic rush coursed through her body. She imagined herself bent over a table, wearing only her heels and stockings, her ass curved out as he slid his glorious, veined cock inside her hot pussy. She could almost feel his meat filling her tight love hole and when she imagined the gush of his warm, wet cream her body shuddered and heaved, the orgasm coming fast and intense as her senses shattered into a million tiny crystals just before floating down to earth.

She took a deep breath and opened her eyes, her gaze resting on the beautiful definition of her thighs before wandering down to her stiletto pumps. She was really glad she bought them the day before.

It was nearly eight in the evening when Anna saw Hector enter the reference section. He seemed to avoid her look until she waved his umbrella. This made him smile and approach her.

She had taken her time getting dressed, choosing a tight, black mini-skirt with a slit on the left side, a matching blazer, and a black thong, the lacy material matching the garters of her black stockings. She pushed back her chair and crossed her legs, as he walked over.

45

'Thank you,' he said, taking the umbrella. He had such a sexy smile. Images of his lips pressed against hers or running up and down her stockings raced through her head as she rested an elbow on the desk, causing her hem to rise just a little bit more. She hoped he noticed everything.

He did.

'I hope you didn't get too wet yesterday,' she responded with a smile.

'I was okay,' he replied, holding out his hand. 'My name is Hector.'

She didn't want to let go of his hand. It was strong yet elegant.

'I'm Anna,' she replied, and noticed the book of erotic French poetry in his hand. 'There's a special collection of her work and some other things you might find interesting.'

'Really? I never knew this place had this kind of material.'

'It's an independent project of mine,' she replied. 'The materials are on the third floor in a storage room. I haven't had the time to catalogue any of it.'

She opened a drawer to take out some keys, her motion causing the hem to rise even higher. From the corner of her eye she could tell he was feasting on the length of her delicious thigh peeking through the slit and the nice way her creamy skin contrasted against her black garter.

'You're welcome to look through it.'

Hector accepted the keys.

She looked him in the eyes.

'Close the door behind you. I'm sure you don't like to be disturbed.'

He gave her a smile, turned and walked towards the elevator.

She waited until the third floor sign lit up. It would take him two minutes to find the room at the end of the hallway, open the door, turn the light on and walk inside.

'Where will he start?' she wondered. 'The illustrated collection of erotic Greek vases? The pictorial Kama Sutra? The Japanese courtesan's guide to oral sex?'

Then she remembered. A sorority mate who now lived in Cairo mailed her some erotic photographs. Anna had spent a good part of last night enjoying pictures of long legged, raven-haired beauties in sexy harem costumes. She especially liked the diaphanous skirts that revealed their pouting thighs and the way the low hems seemed to almost slip off their beautifully curved hips. She had masturbated more than once that night, her orgasms intensified by the sight of hungry lips, velvet stomachs and naked thighs entwined in Sapphic pleasure. The pictures were still on the table next to the shelves.

'He must've seen them by now.' she thought, putting the 'closed' sign on her desk and walking to the elevator.

The tap of her high heels echoed in the empty hallway. She hoped he liked the sound they made. The door was closed.

She found him just as she wished, looking at jewel-eyed nymphs in passionate embraces and gave him a reassuring smile before joining him. The picture he held showed three beauties locked in a passionate embrace. Anna pointed to the one in the middle.

'She went to college with me,' she said. 'Her major was photography. She really gets into her work.' She moved closer and saw the beads of sweat on his forehead.

'Are you hot? I could raise the A.C.'

He set the pictures down and stood close.

47

'Do you like them?' she asked while casually thumbing through the pictures, the heat of his body almost making her swoon.

'Yes. They're very…exciting.'

She pressed her body against him, the bulge in his pants throbbing against her while his fingers caressed her face. She reached up and pressed her lips on his mouth while taking his hands and guiding them down to her buttocks. The sensation of his hands cupping and squeezing her ass as his tongue filled her mouth forced deep moans of pleasure from her throat.

She wanted to consume every inch of his body as she wrapped a leg around his waist, her parted thighs allowing her to feel his bulge against her wet, lacy panties.

They began to pull each other's clothes off. Anna almost ripped off his shirt as she ran her nails over his chest while he undid her skirt and pulled it down, exposing the black stockings and garters she wore on her beautiful legs. His fingers slipped under the thong panty nested in her cleft and slipped into her wet, hungry loins. His touch was gentle, yet firm and sent spasms of pleasure through her body. He massaged the lips of her pussy with his knuckles, moistened his thumb with her juices and gently explored the rim of her anus. She felt an orgasm rise through her spine. In a few seconds his touch made her body quiver in wave after wave of hot ecstasy.

Anna collapsed against Hector's body, bathing in an afterglow of pleasure few lovers or even her beautiful hands had ever given her. Suddenly, she felt a delicious, hungry, craving sensation in her mouth. She dropped to her knees just as he pulled the blouse over her head.

Bare breasted, her nipples brushing against a pair of strong thighs, Anna tugged at his zipper, eager to see the cause of the mouth-watering bulge she craved.

'What a noble looking penis,' she thought, gazing at the engorged member just inches from her lips. She scratched it gently, making him gasp. It was perfectly shaped, straight and tipped by a gland turned deep crimson. She parted her lips slowly and drew him into her mouth, enjoying every delicious inch.

Her fingers travelled over his thighs, up his stomach and scratched his nipples through his shirt. His groans got louder when she tilted her head and took his cock deep inside her throat. She had learned this technique from the Japanese courtesans' guide to oral sex. The times she spent practicing with a banana paid off.

She always liked the way her body looked when she knelt and wished she had a mirror next to them so she could enjoy the curves of her body when she sat with her legs curled under thighs and her beautiful ass resting on her heels. As she sucked away she remembered one time setting a mirror over her head so she could admire her curved buttocks and the sexy way her cleft looked just below her alabaster back.

Suddenly, she felt his strong hands pick her up. She wondered what was on his mind until he sat her on an easy chair by the bookshelves, the cool, leather material feeling so nice on her bare cheeks as he parted her legs and buried his face between her thighs. Anna welcomed his mouth as it feasted on her wet crotch. She pressed her stiletto heels against his back. The second orgasm came even quicker, catching her by surprise. A torrent of pleasure lifting her from the chair, his head locked between her thighs.

She collapsed on the chair, loving the way Hector's tongue ran all over her hips and thighs, just like she imagined, the slight nips he treated the soft, inner part of her thighs to, making her gasp and moan.

It was her turn to surprise him when she turned and stuck her round, hard ass in his face. She always enjoyed the way a black thong made her buttocks appear like two beautiful moons. His deft fingers tugged the thong over as he stood, just before she felt his cock linger outside her pussy, making her reach back and grab one of her cheeks while giving him a wicked, inviting look over her naked shoulder.

A warm, penetrating sensation made Anna's mouth open wide. The walls of her pussy expanded to welcome his thick meat as it pushed deep inside her body. He began sliding in and out vigorously, bringing on that wonderful flood of ecstasy.

This was it. She untied her bun, allowing her black mane to cascade over her shoulders and back. She grabbed a handful and stuffed it in her mouth just as Hector's cum exploded in her loins. Her muffled cries expressed the mind-filling, penetrating orgasm that erupted throughout her body.

His cock lingered for a while inside her pussy. It was so nice to feel his stomach pressing against her ass. He brushed aside her black hair and massaged her naked back, occasionally kissing her sweat-covered, ivory skin, while his other hand slid down to her buttocks and treated her to a nice, firm squeeze.

Later, they got dressed in a hurry. Anna had even tied up her hair again and fixed her make-up but still had the lacy black thong in her hands. She picked up a small book and placed the neatly folded panty in the middle page. She gave it to Hector.

'A bookmark.' Her beautiful hands gestured around the room. 'I need some help reviewing all this material. Could you…assist me?'

He looked at the crammed shelves, held her close, one hand travelling down her naked back and cupping her tight, exquisite cheeks, his finger sliding into her wet cleft and massaging her still juicy pussy and said 'Looks like a very long project…I'd be delighted.'

Exactly one year later Hector and Anna sat in a restaurant to celebrate the anniversary of their first night.

They occupied a booth of the fancy restaurant, Anna in a tight red gown with a waist-high slit and a pair of matching open-toed stiletto heels that allowed Hector to see the gold toe rings he bought her during a sexy weekend in the Florida Keys.

Dinner was a long, sensual affair interspersed with kisses and tender caresses as they fed each other, Hector occasionally making her sigh and sometimes lick his ear as he ran his fingers along her silken inner thighs until he could just feel the heat of her drenched pussy.

'Hello Anna. It's so good to see you again.'

He saw Anna glance behind his back just before a beautiful, raven-haired woman walked up to their table. She wore a green dress that was the exact copy of Anna's except for the keyhole opening that displayed her firm, naked stomach and exposed the hint of her tan line with every step.

Hector's blood rushed from his head when he realized she wore nothing under her gown, just the brief outline of a thong panty.

Anna stood and gave this dark, cinnamon-skinned beauty a swift but tender kiss on the cheek. He recognized her. She was Anna's sexy Egyptian friend, the one who took the erotic harem pictures.

'This is Saphira, the girl who took the photos we…enjoyed,' Anna said, putting her arm around her friend's naked waist.

Saphira flashed him a very sexy smile. Both women stood even closer, their provocative hips touching. Hector's pulse was racing in his body, not knowing, yet anticipating what would happen next. He returned the smile.

'It's a pleasure to meet you,' he said. 'You do excellent work.'

'Thank you,' Saphira responded in a throaty, accented voice.

Anna turned to Saphira. 'Hector has taken some lovely pictures of me.'

'I'd love to see them,' she answered, flashing Hector a coy smile.

'Maybe,' Anna said, 'you'd liked to pose with me.'

Images of Anna and Saphira naked, their arms and thighs wrapped around each other's bodies flashed through his mind. He could picture Anna in her black stockings and black heels and Saphira in white, their lithe, long-legged bodies wrapped around each other.

'Would you like that, baby?' Anna said with a playful, wicked look on her face.

'Maybe we could give you some new ideas?' Saphira asked.

Hector stood and took Anna's hand.

'I'm sure we could come up with something.'

He offered both women an arm and escorted them out, glad for that rainy afternoon when 'Dr Love' had 'struck out'.

Mother Knows Best
by Landon Dixon

When Lucy invited me to a pool party at her house, I thought, well, at least I'll get to see the cute little babe in a bikini. And seeing was all I was likely to get, was all I had got, in two frustrating months of dating the evasive eighteen-year-old. We'd kissed more than a few times, sure, and done some brief, uninspiring tongue-slapping and chest-petting, but that'd been it. Lucy was a great-looking girl – long, chestnut-brown hair, warm, brown eyes, a curvy body enhanced by bouncy, medium-sized jugs and a tight, heart-shaped butt – but she was as skittish about sex as a Mormon at a porn convention.

I arrived at her house around three, and was greeted at the door of the stone-fronted split-level by her sister, Liz – a frumpy, hippy-dippy chick who was perpetually attending the same college as Lucy and I, majoring in Stalinist poetry and bong pottery. 'Hi, Liz,' I said. 'Is Lucy around?'

'Hey, Glen, what's happenin'?' she responded after a few seconds of contemplation, her eyes as empty as the stands at a Strawberry Alarm Clock concert. 'You gonna be at the campus protest tomorrow – to force the science department to free those cockroaches they're experimenting on?'

I tried to slip past the 60's time warp, before it sucked me in and imploded my brain, but the hall was too narrow and she was too wide. 'I doubt it. I've got socks to iron on Monday. Maybe I'll see you at your bail hearing.'

She shoved her rose-tinted granny glasses back up her nose and struggled to process my statement. Then she grinned and said, 'Man, that would be cool, wouldn't it – gettin' busted?'

'It's the only bust you're ever gonna get,' I muttered under my breath. 'I guess Lucy's in the backyard, huh?' I said out loud, putting a swim-move on the road block to rational thought and sliding past her.

I hustled down the hall without looking back, hung a left into a big, airy living room, and then walked to the far wall of the room, which was made entirely of glass. I looked out onto a spacious backyard containing a kidney-shaped swimming pool and recognized Lucy and four of her friends, didn't recognize a brunette babe floating in the pool on a blow-up chair with her back to me. The blue-green water sparkled temptingly under the scorching sun.

Lucy was sitting on the edge of the pool yakking with one of her girlfriends, their feet dangling into the water. She was wearing a tiny, green bikini, her perky tits barely covered by the thin material, her nipples clearly indenting the flimsy boob-holders. Her lustrous brown hair cascaded down her sun-kissed shoulders and back, and her entire body glistened with tanning oil.

I sighed, dreaming of what I could do to that luscious body given half a chance, and rubbed my lengthening cock through my jeans. It was going to be one long, hot afternoon of trying to keep my cool. Then my thoughts of sun and sex, and actual stroking, were interrupted by the

54

startling sound of someone clearing their throat. My hand flew off my hard-on and dove into my pocket, and I whipped my head around. 'Huh!?' I gasped, staring at a woman standing off to my right, in the arched entranceway that connected the kitchen to the dining room. My face went redder than mainland China, and my cock curled up into the foetal position.

'You must be Lucy's boyfriend,' the woman commented, glancing from my crotch to the window, and smiling slightly.

'Uh, yeah…that's right. You're, um, not Lucy's mom, are you?' I spluttered, dreading the answer I knew was coming to that question; you only get one chance to make a first impression on a girl's parents, and mine had been in my pants.

The woman nodded her head, letting the rest of the air out of my ego and erection. 'I'm Leslie,' she said, setting down the paper plates she was carrying on the dining room table and walking over to me, her hand extended.

I took it and shook it, my own mitt as damp and limp as a used condom. 'Uh, nice to meet you, Mrs Brown…Leslie,' I mumbled.

'Lucy's told me so much about you,' she said, cocking her head to one side and studying me from tip to toe. 'And you're just as handsome and muscular as she described.'

'Oh, yeah!?' I gulped, tightening up my chest and arms. 'Well, I do work out every now and then.'

I eyeballed Lucy's mom a little more thoroughly, and quickly confirmed the fact that good looks ran in the family, assuming Liz was adopted, of course. Leslie was a mature, fully filled-out version of Lucy, with the same chestnut hair, brown eyes, pretty face and trim body, but with a chest capacity at least twice as great as her daughter's – her big, heavy-looking tits straining the

55

crimson tank-top she was tightly wearing, her bra-less nipples just about poking holes in the stretched-out fabric. The lady's curvaceous lower body was spray-painted with faded blue jeans, and her face and arms and shoulders were tanned a deep-dish brown. She sort of looked like Adrienne Barbeau, circa Cannibal Women in the Avocado Jungle of Death, and I stared at her awesome cleavage and succulent jugs like I was staring into the Grand Canyon for the very first time.

'It sure looks like you do,' Leslie said, bringing me back to reality for a moment, but only for a moment, because then she came closer and rubbed my bare arm with her soft, warm, brown hand.

'You've got a nice body, too…for a single mom,' I blurted, not being the greatest small-talker in the world when there were big doings in my pants. Lucy had told me that her father had passed away two years ago.

Leslie ran a thick, pink tongue over her full, scarlet-painted lips. 'Why thank you, Glen,' she said, stroking my arm. She looked out the sliding glass doors that led to the pool. 'Lucy can be a little…distant, can't she?' I peeled my eyes off the gorgeous MILF's rising and falling breast-basket and glanced out at the partygoers, not exactly sure what Leslie meant. 'Uh, yeah. We haven't…done anything, if that's what you mean?'

Lucy's mom reached out and turned the lock on the door. 'That's what I thought, poor baby,' she breathed. She leaned back against the glass and looked up into my saucered eyes. 'I don't know where she gets that from; I'm not like that at all. When I see something I like, I go for it.'

And with that stunning confession out of the way, the forty-something honey with the Hollywood body grabbed my shoulders and planted a soft one bang-on my pucker.

Holy shit! my addled brain screamed, this sexy, mature mama wanted it, me – bad! She hungrily kissed me a couple more times, in a most unmotherly-like fashion, and then I shook the rust off my synapses and put my arms into motion, wrapped them around her red-hot body and kissed her right back.

We sucked face like a couple of horny high-school kids, even though the busty lady had a good twenty-five years on my nineteen. She darted her tongue into my mouth and aroused my own sleeping giant tongue into action, and we started French kissing like it was springtime in Paris, bridging the generation gap via the universal language of lust.

I caught my breath and opened my eyes, looked out the window at Lucy dipping her toes into the pool and chattering away to her friends, and suddenly, shockingly remembered our southern exposure. 'Mrs…I mean Leslie, Lucy – her friends – are going to see us!' I yelped.

Leslie looked at me with her liquid brown eyes and smiled, tiny crow's feet appearing at the sides of her mouth and eyes. 'Don't worry, sweetheart,' she said, 'these windows are so heavily-tinted that when the sun is shining on them no one can possibly see what's going on inside the house.'

I gazed down at her lightly-freckled treasure chest, out at Lucy, and then slipped my hands under the top of Leslie's top and pulled her big, brown jugs out of the skin-tight garment. Her incredible tits hung huge and heavy, sagging only a little, her chocolate-dipped nipples – the same milk nubs that Lucy had sucked as a child – jutting a good, solid, rubbery inch out from her silver dollar-sized aureoles.

I pondered the beauty of her dangling double-D's for awhile, my cock a hardened steel rod in my pants, my

57

mind racing back to earliest childhood memories of Kindergarten – chewing on sweet, delicious cookies and then washing them down with frothy, white milk, before hitting the blue blanket for a well-deserved nap. Looking at Leslie's well-slung titties was like actually seeing the naked boobs of your ultra-hot high school Spanish teacher – the one you imagined tit-fucking while you jerked off in the semi-privacy of your family's bathroom.

Leslie broke into my wet daydreams by pulling her top up over her head and tossing it aside, leaving her sun-burnished upper body as bare as my need. 'What are you waiting for, Glen?' she asked softly, her ponderous boobs trembling deliciously when she shrugged her buff shoulders.

I instantly grabbed onto her ample tits, cupped them, squeezed and kneaded them, revelled in the hot, smooth feel of her swollen boobies. These weren't tiny little teen titties, bumps on some skinny skank's girlish chest; these were big, bold woman breasts, over-ripe melons that had, no doubt, seen plenty of action, and would see, and feel, plenty more.

'Suck my tits!' Leslie groaned as I felt up her pliable mams, closing her eyes and leaning back against the thin, tinted glass that separated fantasy from reality.

Through the looking-glass, I could see Lucy toss a beach ball to some guy in the pool, playing innocent and carefree under the blazing sun, while her wicked mother was playing for sexual keeps only fifty feet away, her lewd, nude boobs clasped in my hands. I swallowed my Adam's apple, bent my head down, and stuck out my tongue and tentatively flicked it against one of Leslie's engorged nipples. Her tits jerked in my hands, her body slammed against the window, and she moaned, her breasts obviously very, very sensitive.

I gripped the lady's jugs more firmly in my sweaty paws and swirled my tongue all over her inflamed nipples – licking circles around first one fully-flowered nip, and then the other. Her tit-peaks grew even larger as I teased them, slobbered them with my spit. Then I sucked a burnt-sugar nipple into my mouth and pulled on it.

'Yes, Glen, yes!' the squirming, full-bodied mother of two cried out, grabbing my head and riffling her fingers through my short, blond hair.

I sucked hard on her distended nipple, her tit, looking up into her lust-misted eyes, massaging her massive hooters with my hands as I suckled at her breast. I swallowed more and more of her tit, until I had a good, solid half of her mammary sealed between my lips, excitedly tugging on it like I expected to draw warm, wet nourishment. Then I disgorged the sopping wet tit and sucked up her other tit, repeated the same erotic process, thoroughly enjoying the taste and texture of her round, brown mounds.

Leslie eventually pulled my face off her chest with a soggy pop and ripped my t-shirt out of my jeans, tugged it up my torso and over my head as I hastily raised my arms. The experienced babe's eyes were wild, and she ran her hands all over my smooth, bare chest, scratching me with her long, blood-red talons. She grabbed onto my pecs and started tongue-lashing my nipples, her tongue warm and wet and insistent. She licked and sucked and bit my hardened nips, her nostrils flaring, her moist breath steaming against my tingling skin. She clawed at my belt, my zipper, and before I could even react by egging her on, she'd reached inside my pants and trunks and pulled out my cock.

'Fuck, yeah, Mrs Brown!' I hollered, the 'Mrs' making things all the more sexy.

She dropped to her knees and tugged my rock-hard dong all the way out of my jeans, jerking me forward as she did so, and then she started stroking. Fuck, but that turned-on babe's sure, hot hand felt great on my pipe! Her smooth palm rubbed up and down my throbbing pole, driving me crazy, hand-forging my steel to an awesome length and rigidity.

'What a beautiful cock you have,' she breathed, her red-tipped digits sliding back and forth on my prick. 'It seems to really respond to a mother's touch.'

Sweet Jesus! The over-endowed MILF was talking dirty and everything! This cock-crazy mama was sure as hell nothing like the typical mothers of the girls I dated; they were usually thick-waisted broads with prison-issue haircuts, Harry Carey bifocals, and as much sex appeal as Rosanne Barr.

I popped the button on my jeans open and slid my pants and swimsuit down to my ankles, to give the sexed-up beauty even better access to my wiener and beans, and she quickly cradled my tightened nut sack in her left hand while she jacked my meat with her right. She dexterously juggled my balls with her slender fingers, rubbed my shaft with long, sensuous strokes intermixed with quicker, harder hand-tugs, the silver bands on her thumbs flashing.

My body quivered with delight, and just when I thought it couldn't get any better than having my girlfriend's mother jerk me off while my girl frolicked in a bikini in the blistering background, Leslie put my piece in her personal piece de resistance by seizing my prick at the base and tonguing my hood. 'Yeah, suck my cock, Mrs Brown!' I groaned, my knees buckling with the sexual weight of the well-aged brunette lashing at my bloated cock-top with her slippery tongue.

She swirled her tongue all around my cock-head, then bounced it up and down on her cushiony, pink pleasure tool. I clutched her silky hair and pulled her face closer, and she swallowed my cap without hesitation and began a raunchy ride down my shaft. Her full lips slid easily down my straining dick, her mouth stretching wide to allow her to smoothly and wetly inhale my meat. Years and years of practice and polish had obviously taught Leslie the kind of techniques I'd thought only existed in porn videos and locker-room urban legends, because she rapidly gobbled up my cock until her nose pushed into my pubes and she had my entire prick buried in her mouth and throat.

My legs shook uncontrollably, the feeling of hot, tight wetness incredible! This definitely wasn't the half-hearted suck, gag, and spit of the typical grossed-out teenager; this was hardcore, heavy-duty deep-throating at its most seriously erotic. And it was too much for me to handle. 'I'm gonna come!' I shouted.

Leslie stared up at me with her glittering, brown eyes, her nostrils billowing, her throat constricting, making no move whatsoever to release my long, hard cock from her stuffed air passage. I threw back my head, grunted with joy, and blasted creamy sperm down that wicked MILF's gulping throat. I came again and again, my body jerking with each and every cum-blast, Leslie taking it all in. And when I'd rocketed my last gooey snowball directly into her stomach, I stroked her thick, lustrous hair and promised, 'I come quick, baby, but I come often.' It was a special talent of mine.

She slowly disgorged my dripping meat, slid my entire dong out of her talented mouth and throat and stroked its slimy length with her hand again. 'If that's the case, sweetheart, why don't you stick this handsome thing of yours in my pussy?' she suggested.

I eagerly nodded my head. And as my glistening, stay-hard cock twitched excitedly, anxious for the warmth of a new sex-hole, Leslie stood up and spun around so that she was facing out towards the pool. She unzipped her form-fitting jeans and eased them over her big, round butt, bending forward to slide the faded blue pants the rest of the way down her shiny, suntanned legs. She was wearing as little underwear on her bottom as she'd been wearing on her top – which is to say, none.

She winked at me over her shoulder, a saucy smile on her pouting lips, and then she lifted her bare feet out of the puddled pants and placed her hands on the glass and spread her legs. She stood on her tip-toes, her back arched, her brazen butt thrust out and swaying from side to side, tempting me like a red flag tempts a raging bull.

I jerked my running shoes out of my jeans and rushed forward, grabbed her oh-so-grabbable ass and squeezed her taut cheeks, my heart racing at two hundred beats a minute, my cock fully inflated. She laughed as I enthusiastically kneaded her pliable bottom, then grew a whole hell of a lot serious by saying, 'Fuck me, Glen! We'll watch Lucy and her cute little friends splash around outside while you jam that big, ever-ready cock of yours into my wet cunt and fuck me senseless!' She pushed her bronze bum further back, spread her legs wider, and I gripped my slick prick with one hand, her waist with the other, and shoved my cock-head into her slippery labes. I pushed my hood through Leslie's soft folds and into her dripping snatch, only vaguely hearing the sound of voices and music, laughter and splashing, coming from some outside world that I was no longer a part of.

She moaned, grabbed onto her hanging tits with one hand while keeping her other hand plastered against the glass. 'Fuck me, Glen!' she pleaded. 'Fuck me like you'd like to fuck my daughter!'

I sucked heated air into my billowing lungs and plunged my dong deep inside her gash, driving it balls-deep into her juicy cunt. Then I grabbed hold of her waist and started churning my hips, started fucking the overwrought mother.

'Yes!' Leslie cried, her head hanging down, both hands splayed against the thin see-through partition that separated us from civilized society.

I pumped my engorged cock in and out of her amazingly tight twat, moving my hips faster and faster, sweat coating my face and body as I pounded the heavenly MILF's ass. The sliding door shook in its frame as I hammered Leslie with my dick, my body smacking hard against her rippling bum, my prick sawing rapidly back and forth in her gripping cooze. Outside, Lucy stood on the diving board and glanced at the window behind which her boyfriend and mother were wildly fucking, like she'd heard something, but then she adjusted the thin straps on her bikini top, felt her titties to make sure they were covered, and dived into the water.

'I'm gonna come!' I bleated for a second time that sultry afternoon, slamming Leslie's puss like a man possessed.

'No!' she yelled, pasting her sweat-sheened body up against the glass so that my dick popped out of her puss. She whipped her head around, her hair flying, and stared desperately at me. 'I want you to fuck me in the ass!'

She wanted it all – all in one session! And I wasn't about to argue with her; I'd always been taught to respect my elders. I mumbled, 'You got it,' and watched in awe as she reached behind her and spread her butt cheeks, serving up her sun-burnished bum for our mutual enjoyment.

I spat into my hand, used my saliva and her cunt juices to lube my pulsating dick, and then glanced uncertainly back and forth between my plumped-out prick and her tiny, puckered butt-hole. Just how the fuck was I going to jam my fire-forged, seven-inch shaft into that teeny little opening, I wondered? I was about to question the lusty mom about the impossible physics of the situation, to save her certain abuse, when she hissed, 'Stick your cock up my ass and fuck me! Now!'

Her fingers clawed at her cheeks, pulling herself apart, her knuckles burning white on the tight, tanned flesh, and I concluded that perhaps all things were sexually possible in our over-aroused state. I hoped so, anyway. I gamely clutched my cock and shoved its angry, purple hood up against her starfish. I pushed hard, and, to my astonishment, my grossly swollen knob punched into her bung without too much difficulty. She pushed back at me, sinking my raging prick into her tremulous ass like a spear into the warm, wet earth.

I recklessly ploughed forward, till my front-side made contact with her backside, and the entire length of my dong was buried inside her gripping chute. I restarted that good, old pumping rhythm, and marvelled at how smoothly my swollen cock slid back and forth in the sweet lady's stretched-out anus.

'Fuck, yes,' she whimpered, her hands off her bum now and squeaking up and down on the window pane as I banged her bottom. Then she sent one of her hands down to her cunt, to urgently rub her clit.

I torqued up the sexual pressure a couple more notches, furiously pounded my prick into Leslie's butt-hole, mother-fucking her jiggling bottom again and again and again, till my balls tightened with fevered anticipation and the whole depraved, white-hot situation became way too intense for me. 'I'm coming!' I bellowed.

'Cum in my ass!' Leslie screamed back, frantically polishing her button, the two of us not giving a flying fuck now if a sudden cloudburst sent the gang by the pool scurrying inside the house for shelter, to witness our frenzied anal-coupling for themselves.

I desperately plundered Leslie's ass a few more times, staring with glazed eyes at her young daughter, as she climbed out of the pool and smoothed back her long, damp hair. Then I blew a sexual fuse and blasted sizzling jizz deep into that coming mother's bottom. I came hard and long, as she did, the both of us howling our ecstasy. I filled her trembling derriere with what felt like gallons of heated sperm, until I blew a final stiff, sticky salute to her over-ripe beauty and collapsed on top of her, drained of all feeling, grabbing onto her jugs for support.

It was only when we were shakily putting ourselves back together, that space cadet Liz wandered into the funky-smelling room and asked, 'Hey, are you guys okay? I thought I heard somethin'.'

Leslie assured her daughter that everything was better than fine, and Liz shrugged her doughy shoulders and sauntered into the kitchen in search of munchies.

I glanced out the window and noticed someone tumble out of an inflatable chair and into the pool – the woman I hadn't recognized earlier. But when she turned around, she revealed the dripping-wet, jaw-dropping fact that she was the full-figured, equally mature duplicate of the mother I'd just fucked.

'Maybe you'd like to meet my sister?' Leslie asked, holding my hand as we watched the glistening vision of loveliness climb out of the pool.

The growing bulge in my jeans was my response.

Changing Objectives
by Jeremy Edwards

Alison shivered slightly as the muggy sidewalk gave way to the climate-controlled foyer. The cool air felt refreshing against her bare legs, and she was glad she'd chosen to wear a skirt. She had wanted to dress up a little, anyway. Though this was primarily a test of her mental acuity and general knowledge, she had to assume that the staff of *Think!* also had their eyes open for potential contestants who looked beautiful, cuddly, or stylish. Alison didn't think of herself as 'beautiful,' and she was more the skinny than the 'cuddly' type. But on a good day, she calculated that she could manage 'stylish'. So she'd donned an elegant, mid-length floral skirt, and a teal jersey that flattered her sharp shoulders and small, pointed breasts. She had crowned herself with a pair of retro-chic sunglasses that she knew would stay in place astride her auburn bangs, if she avoided sudden head movements.

Alison's elegance was a bohemian sort of elegance, and stockings were usually out of the question. On some days even panties were out of the question. But today being a sticky one, Alison had thought better of that option. After all, it might not impress the game show staff if she showed up for her test with her nice floral skirt glued to the crack of her ass, courtesy of the relative humidity.

'May I help you?' asked the receptionist.

'Yes, I'm here for the 4:00 test for *Think!*' said Alison. She projected confidence, but she had to admit to herself that she had a few rare-and-exotic butterflies in her stomach. She hoped she'd be able to relax sufficiently for concentrating on the test. She wondered if she ought to have made a point of masturbating that morning, instead of spending quite so much time boning up on history, geography, and basic science. She knew that all her cramming wouldn't do her any good if she couldn't approach the questions in the right frame of mind, and she further knew that a good twenty minutes of self-pleasuring usually kept her relaxed and happy for hours afterward.

'You're early,' said the receptionist. 'You can have a seat in the lobby until they call you.'

Early, Alison reflected. As she took a seat, she noticed that there were restrooms right along the far wall of the lobby, in the familiar company of a payphone and a water fountain. She wondered if perhaps it wasn't too late to redress her neglect. It wouldn't be a leisurely pussy-pampering session like at home; but she had done some lovely things for herself in bathroom stalls in the past. Doing her own oyster in a strange, almost-public place made everything happen faster, and sometimes even better. She squeezed her thighs together, involuntarily, as she considered the prospect.

She was startled out of this train of thought when a tall young woman crossed into her peripheral vision from around a corner. The woman, a magnificent-looking twenty something blonde in a sleek, navy-blue skirt suit, wore a 'STAFF' badge on a lanyard and carried a clipboard. The woman seemed to break her stride for just an instant, as if looking Alison over, before making her way across the lobby. As she drew near, Alison could see that she had a friendly smile on her face.

'May I have your name, please?' The woman spoke softly but crisply. Alison noticed that she had some sort of becoming northern European accent.

Alison felt the butterflies flutter again as she answered. 'I'm Alison Lloyd.'

The woman made a check mark on her clipboard. 'Hello, Alison. I'm Inge. I think they'll be ready for you shortly.' Inge smiled pleasantly again before walking briskly out of sight.

Alison knew at this point that she had better not disappear into the ladies' room for that quick treat. It was really too bad, because her brief consideration of this option had already had an effect on her intimate physiology. She could feel the resulting wetness in her panties, which were now clinging against her pussy. It was a nice feeling, though, and in its own way it made her feel less nervous. While she compulsively reviewed her state capitals and multiplication tables one more time, the hint of wetness down there was a soothing reminder that life is not all in the brain.

'Ms Lloyd?'

Alison's heart jumped, because she hadn't seen him approaching her. The suave, handsome man extending his hand had evidently entered the lobby while she had been looking in the other direction.

'I'm Gavin,' he said, as she rose to shake his hand. She saw herself smoothing her skirt down in that fidgety manner she couldn't help assuming sometimes.

Wow, he was gorgeous, she noted as she met his charismatic glance. His features were perhaps a little too quirky to make him look like a model or movie star, but

69

they embodied a charm that set him apart from all the ordinary-looking guys. His thick, straight brown hair curled seductively under each ear, and his strong eyebrows were softened by laughing eyes and a sensitive mouth. Like Inge, he wore a name badge.

'I'll be giving you your test today,' he told her. There was something about the way his eyes lingered over her face and her body that sent a chill – not unpleasant – from her ankles up to her clinging panties. Whereas Inge had seemed to be sizing her up from a distance, Gavin's assessment was done from less than a foot away, and felt almost tangible. Alison's balance of mind and matter was now veering away from its midpoint – the soft, wet matter between her legs was increasingly drawing her concentration away from the mental challenge ahead.

'We'll be in the first conference room on the right,' Gavin said. His eyes twinkled at her for a moment. Then he began to escort her down the short corridor.

In the conference room, he ushered her to a seat at the far end of a long wooden table. In front of her were a manila folder and a pencil. Her chair was comfortably padded, and the perfectly-air-conditioned climate of the room felt delicious.

Gavin closed the door and walked to the end of the table nearest him. 'Any questions before you begin?' he asked, kindly.

Alison wanted to ask him all sorts of questions – questions about whether she could undo various parts of his clothing and touch him in all kinds of places – but she merely shook her head to indicate 'No'.

'Go ahead, then, whenever you're ready,' said Gavin.

With trembling fingers, she opened the folder. Ten questions jumped out at her, ten easy questions…ten questions whose answers she knew yesterday, knew this morning…and could not, for the life of her, bring up now. 'What is the capital of New Zealand?' 'What is the atomic number of calcium?' 'What is meant by the term *andante,* in musical notation?' Alison simply couldn't concentrate. Her pussy was throbbing for attention, her focus had been totally diverted by the presence of this appetizing guy, and her legs were tingling from the kisses of the air-conditioned air.

For five intense minutes, she struggled to call up the information she should have had at her disposal. She filled in every blank, but she knew most of the answers were probably wrong.

'Okay, Alison, your time is up,' said Gavin. Alison welcomed this announcement. Clearly, this was a lost cause.

She stood up and walked to Gavin's end of the table. 'I'm afraid I didn't do as well as I should have,' she confessed. She handed him her folder.

It only took him seconds to scan her answers and score her performance. His face seemed to sag. Then he looked up, and his eyes met hers. 'This happens sometimes,' he said. 'Would you like another chance? I think we have an opening tomorrow.'

She eagerly accepted, and her heart was fluttering as she scurried back through the lobby. Just as she approached the exit, Inge caught up with her.

'I am so glad to know you'll be back,' said Inge, touching Alison very lightly on the elbow. 'Gavin was so disappointed that you didn't qualify today.'

Alison knew what she had to do.

When she arrived at the studio the next day, almost everything was the same. She had sweated her way through similar weather, wearing a similar outfit. This time, however, one article of clothing had been left at home. And, just as she had predicted, her thin skirt was clinging to the crack of her panty-free ass. Yet today she didn't mind. It felt sexy.

Another difference was that where she had arrived empty-handed yesterday, today she was clutching a manila folder.

In the lobby, Inge greeted her like she was an old friend. 'Welcome back, Alison. Gavin will be ready for you in a moment.'

Will he really be ready for me? Alison wondered. As she waited for her cue, she sizzled with a different sort of nervousness from her pre-exam jitters of the day before. Today she had no thoughts of a quick fingering in a bathroom stall. She was horny, all right. But she had higher aspirations than a date with herself in the john.

When he came to collect her, Gavin's face struck her as even kinder and, if it was possible, more handsome than on the previous occasion. Alison hoped she wasn't imagining it when she noted that he looked genuinely glad to see her.

He led her to the same conference room, and she took her place at the same end of the table. Then, she pushed aside the manila folder that awaited her there, and substituted her own.

'Oh, I'm sorry, Alison,' said Gavin. 'You're not allowed to bring any materials into the –'

She felt her nervousness evaporate as she interrupted him, and she delivered her words with a mischievous smile. This was it. 'I brought my own test today,' she explained.

She laughed inside when she saw the look of boyish confusion crossed Gavin's adorable features. 'Your own test? I don't –'

Alison put her finger to her lips and opened her folder. 'This will just take a minute,' she assured him.

While she quickly filled out the form she had prepared, she was aware that Gavin was watching her. A glance in his direction revealed that his mouth hung open in an expression of perplexity. But his eyes seemed to burn with something else – something intoxicating, something that made her acutely aware of the rude but sensuous way her skirt was caressing her ass crack, and the titillating breath of the climate-controlled air around her bare ankles.

She finished in just a minute, as promised, and handed him the form. Since she knew it by heart, having rehearsed it over and over in her mind last night while stroking herself under the covers, she could follow along as he silently read:

1. Do you find your examiner sexually attractive?
Yes

2. Are you wearing panties?
No

3. Do you have to be anywhere in a hurry after this test?
No

4. Do you have any aversion to undressing handsome men in conference rooms?
No

5. Do you have any aversion to sprawling across conference room tables while you're brought to thunderous orgasms?
No

Gavin let the document fall to the floor. He seemed frozen for a moment, his face a cartoon of incredulous anticipation. It was the work of a moment for Alison to take him in her arms

'I realize anyone can walk in here and *claim* not to be wearing panties,' she breathed in his ear. 'So of course I understand that the staff must verify any such claim.' She took his hand and guided it under her skirt.

'Verify, baby, verify,' she urged.

She felt his fingers begin to explore her, sending sparks in every direction. This was all it took to instigate a delicious mini-climax, and she sighed as her cunt showered Gavin's fingers with honey.

He looked in her eyes. He seemed concerned. 'Please understand…no matter what we do now, it doesn't mean that I can get you on the show. I don't do those kinds of favours.'

She almost thought she would cry, he was so sweet. Instead, she laughed. 'I'm not thinking about the show. I want favours from you, all right, but not the kind you're talking about.'

Gavin's face relaxed into an expression of delirious joy. She pulled his weight toward her and let herself slouch onto the table. Her sunglasses fell off her head, but she didn't care. 'Do me a favour, Gavin,' she coaxed. 'Do me a big favour, right in my sweet spot, right here on the table.'

If this had happened yesterday, she might have proceeded more slowly, by delicately offering her nipples to his lips. But after twenty-four hours of dripping with lust for this man, she wanted his cock up her skirt as soon as humanly possible. So she found his zipper, and, within seconds, she was guiding his warm, firm flesh inside her.

'I wanted you yesterday,' Gavin confided as they began to squirm together. 'But I was afraid that a little manila folder would keep us apart.'

Alison giggled. 'As I see it, the only things that are going to be kept apart are my legs.' She closed her eyes as the deepest thrust yet set her tingling. He leaned into her, grabbing gently but passionately at the undersides of her knees, and she felt him dotting her nose and cheeks with the softest of kisses. Each little peck nudged her upwards, raising her closer to ecstasy on silken layers of joy, which she writhed upon like an animal.

His breath was warm and pleasantly nutty across her face. They must drink flavoured coffee here, she thought, just as an orgasmic tide surged through her and pushed all thoughts away. Gavin's hot brew kissed her insides in gorgeous, pumping spurts, and she boiled with pleasure as he shuddered against her.

Eventually, Alison sat up and began to tidy herself. Gavin was grinning.

'Inge will be happy,' he said.

Alison thought of the friendly blonde, the gorgeous woman who had gazed at her, smiled at her, and welcomed her. 'Inge?'

'Yeah, she sort of looks out for me. Like a sister. She could tell right away that I was longing for…well, *this.*'

For reasons she couldn't account for, Alison suddenly wondered if Inge's relationship with Gavin was always entirely sisterly. And she wondered if Inge's warmth toward *her* had been tinged with anything besides natural friendliness and concern for Gavin. Perhaps, Alison reflected, her next conference with Gavin could include the alluring Inge as well…

'What are you thinking about?' Gavin asked.

'About the next time I take the test,' Alison replied, with a sparkle in her voice.

Don't Quote Me
by Lynne Jamneck

Sometimes it's like chrome. Sleek and shiny on the surface. When you see it, without really looking, you don't notice the nickel underneath the plate is silver. All you take in is the gleam.

It was like that with Wendy.

If I'd seen her in a club or a bar, her sparkle would probably have faded into the nightlife background. As it was, it was 8 am in the morning, on a Thursday. I'm not usually awake this early, but my insomnia makes an appearance in quarterly bouts, and so, yes; I was having trouble sleeping.

I was feeling up the day-old bread when she turned the corner of the candy isle and came to stand close to me. Too close, I thought, to merely be inspecting the dough. She wore a black DKNY dress and something sparkled around her neck. In the harsh lights of the 7-Eleven she looked hyper real.

She looked at me. 'White or brown?'

'Not sure myself. They're not fresh.'

She inspected the loaves. 'I have to eat. Which would you take?'

That was pretty much the last coherent thing she asked me. It might have been a simple request for me to help her with an easy choice, but her eyes were looking me over like I was steak.

Her red SLK was parked out front. She was probably a good eight or ten years older than me. Her apartment was beachfront slick. High walls, infra-red and glass everywhere.

Wendy was one of those women who could bring the fuck out in you simply by being too close. I let her take me home because of exactly that. She'd asked me about bread and all I could think about was her nipples in my mouth. I forgot to lock my car before we left the 7-Eleven.

Inside, her house was shiny too. Kitchen-chromed, wood polished and heavy furniture. It was all very butch. I sensed testosterone.

'Don't worry,' she said from the opposite end of the kitchen. 'He's away on business. Your bourbon. Drink.'

We fucked in her bed. Neither of us were very verbal, but when she wrapped those long gorgeous legs around my waist and in due course begged me not to stop, I crashed and called her something dirty.

We had sex in her kitchen again before I left. She was getting something to drink and I surprised her from behind. She spilt milk on the floor.

Wendy was sleek, but ultimately cold. Maybe it was because it was July, and the middle of winter.

God help me.

Have you ever felt so hard that it seemed your insides would supernova at the sound of her voice? Implode with too much of everything? When you accidentally brush against her skin in the kitchen as she takes the soda bottle from your hand, or laughs at one of your clever jokes?

When I was seventeen the world could either end or begin with a kiss.

Shawn moved in next door with her parents and one older brother when I was fifteen. She had careless hair and eyes like burnished wood. A lackadaisical attitude and a crooked smile that made you want to act criminal.

The attraction was there from the very first day. I helped her carry a box of vinyl records from the moving van up to her room on the second floor. It was spring. Fresh.

Two years later, after the vinyl. Shawn and I were draped on my mother's couch, playing some manhandled version of our own private charades when something happened. A fumble. A suppressed exploit. What I remember next was the chilly feel of the lemonade bottle in my hand, trying not to drop it on the carpet and my eyes closed; Shawn's mouth on mine and her hair smelling of apricots. She smelled like a girl on the verge of becoming something else. Her smell was like my own. Somehow I must have set down the bottle of soda. We were lying down on the couch, Shawn on top and never in my wildest dreams could I have imaged that a lanky girl like her could feel so heavy. Our lust scared and excited in equal measure. We lay on that couch kissing for what felt like days, weeks. Sometimes, especially when I had to speak in front of people, my tongue felt alien in my own mouth. When Shawn kissed me there was nothing foreign; nothing that could make me hide from myself.

We kissed and fumbled a summer, autumn and winter away; in my bedroom, in hers, at the top of the stairs with her mother watching Oprah in the living room and the sound turned up high. I took her virginity in the backseat of her brother's Volvo. I had no idea she was that inexperienced.

That's how I will always remember spring. The warmth of the butterfly-sun on Shawn's back as I ran my hand up her shirt, cornered away in the backyard and the balm of the evening air as our breath fogged up the backseat windows. We were kids back then. But we were kids on the verge of something bigger.

The first time we made love I knew part of me would cling to her forever. I'd hoped that the opposite would also be true.

I was a struggling writer masquerading as an author of worth. I first saw her in the library. She was checking out a copy of *Arabian Nights* which I found to be such a literary turn-on that the rest of me was immediately piqued as well.

I chatted her up with the help of my best opening line. It must have been good, because she laughed. She was impressed by my knowledge of Persia and the Sassanid Queen. Her name was Sarah. Like Scheherazade, but different.

Sarah was deeply sensual. God, she took her time when we had sex. She had a way of slowing me down when I threatened to take the heat between us and run. She could build it up by making me relax, making me feel every moment.

Sarah had a thing. She liked licking the faint trail of sweat from my back that would inevitably rise there. She'd coat her tongue with the salty tang and turn me around for a kiss, letting me taste myself. I kept telling her that it wasn't all me. That I'd mixed with her tongue and her lips and the inside of her mouth imbued with her breath.

Sometimes she reminded me of Shawn. Moments of suavity, riddled with unexpected vulnerability. Sarah also frightened me. She made me want to be someone I wasn't. Someone I didn't think was a part of me.

That's why I cheated on her. Because I was a coward and didn't want to face up to the person I could be. It was perverse.

I brought home a mirror-image of myself. Butch dyke. Shitkicker boots and a hard-on that never let up. We were fucking in the hallway when I saw Sarah. We hadn't heard her come in. She was supposed to be in Detroit for the week-end. She just looked at me. Whatever-her-name-was had her face turned to the wall and didn't see anything. Her grunts filled the tight morning air. I didn't stop. For me to not be hurt I had to be colder.

I haven't seen Sarah since.

I doubt whether even the smallest piece of me remains remotely close to her. The same cannot be said of her influence over me.

Live and learn. It's true. You can't live and *not* pick up something useful; if so, you're doing it wrong. Trust me.

The bad news is that, even when you learn, that doesn't mean you won't repeat the same mistakes again. And probably more than once.

It's winter again. We'll see what happens.

I Say His Name Out Loud
by Adrie Santos

In one scenario, I walk into his office to find him sitting, tired. The late nights are obviously catching up with him, his head laid on the hard mahogany desk top, his breath deep and heavy in sleep.

I watch him for a moment, taking note of the tiny little hairs that run along the back of his long neck, the way his black hair remains perfectly in place even though his head has fallen down into rest, and the sound of his breath.

I focus on his hands lying on the desk next to his head – his wrists also adorned with tiny black hairs that lead to his hands which, though not very large, appear strong and masculine.

I can feel the familiar longing building in me as I stare at what I consider to be one of the most delicious beings on Earth. Since the first moment I laid eyes in him, as he stood in the back of the crowd of suits on one of my first days on the job I have felt it – an intense want that can barely be described. I was introduced to the suits, one by one, anxiously awaiting my chance to meet the mysterious man with the deepest eyes I'd ever seen who stood at the back of the group looking right into me, but the introduction never came.

As they walked away I turned back to give him one last smile – he was still looking. I moved down the corridor barely able to control my knees from trembling. Only weeks later did I find out that he was one of my bosses – Edward.

I begin to turn away from him and back towards the door, the nurturing side of me not wanting to disturb him from his much-needed rest, but I stop myself – I need one last look. I move in closer, inching my way towards him until I am standing right next to him. My heart races and I reach my hand out to him.

My fingers tremble as I place my hand gently on his back, my insides fluttering wildly at the mere feel of the white cotton of his shirt. I can't help myself – I begin to run my finger tips along his back, savouring the feel of him. He sighs and it startles me – but not enough to move my hand away – I can't. I continue to touch him and the longing only increases with each slide of my hand.

With his head now slightly turned to the side, still pressed against the desk, I lean in bringing my face close to the back of his neck. I can see that my breath against his skin is causing the tiny little hairs to stand on their ends – is he aware of my presence?

Though scared at how he may react, I can't stop myself – I am strangely intoxicated by the smell of his skin, and excited at the subtle way that his body is reacting to my touch, causing me to lean in even closer until my lips are resting softly on his skin.

Placing tiny kisses on the back of his neck, the little hairs feel good as they prickle my lips. With each light kiss, he stirs, and I notice his breathing begin to change. In my excitement, I am unaware that my own breath is also changing – becoming faster and louder.

My lips inch towards his ear, my chest and hands are now pressed against his back, and I immediately see goose bumps form on his beautiful face. His eyes open, but show no sign of protest or even surprise – did he know it was me all along?

He raises his head off the desk and our eyes lock in a gaze, our faces so close that I can for the first time since we met almost a year ago really see into his deep-set eyes. I wait, almost in fear that he is going to ask me to stop and remind me how unprofessional I am being, but he says nothing and I take it as a silent go-ahead. Our faces move together almost as if in slow motion until my lips are finally resting on his.

It isn't long before I am completely lost in his kiss, our lips and tongues moving together perfectly, and our breaths drowning out the buzzing of the office lights. As if doing a dance, we move about, holding each other tight until we are standing behind his desk. He presses hard against me, his lips never moving from mine, and I lean back until I am practically sitting on the desk. My body is aching – I feel as if I need to get even closer to him. I am consumed by him and by my feelings for him – feelings that I have longed to act on for what seemed like an eternity. He stops me for a second and just looks at me with the same familiar glare that has both intimidated and attracted me all of this time, and in typical Edward tone, his voice deep, he asks, 'What are we doing?'

And in typical me-style, I smile, 'Who cares,' quickly putting an end to the possibility of any doubt by pressing my lips back to his, with my tongue following.

His hands move almost shyly down my shoulders, slowly inching their way toward my breasts. I laugh to myself, recognizing his 'But I am your boss' type caution, and decide to help him along by bringing his fingers to the buttons of my blouse. He hesitates, causing me to open my eyes and pull my lips away ever so slightly, and flashes me a naughty grin – his dark brows raise and lower in amusement before he proceeds. Within seconds, his fingers are working away at my buttons, and finally exposing my white lace bra. I hear him moan ever so quietly as he takes a moment to glance down at my tanned heaving chest with my nipples peeking through the delicate fabric. I feel myself drip with excitement at watching him enjoy my ample offerings. He lowers his head and brings his mouth to my breasts as his hand gently pulls the lace to the side.

He doesn't break our gaze as he begins to slowly lick tiny little circles around my pert nipple. My whole body quivers in a delight that can only be imagined. I don't know what is more arousing – his tongue finally on my skin where it belongs, or his stare, so intense and unable to break even for a moment from mine. If only he realized how much I crave him and all of the things that I would allow him to do to me.

I resume my fantasy; he is still lapping away at my nipples, staring deep into my eyes. I can't help but moan softly. I take his face in my hands and pull his lips back to mine, whispering into them, 'I want you inside me.'

I proceed to move my hands down to his belt, tearing away at the leather, the buckle, and finally the zipper. The anticipation as I reach in to claim what I have so longed for is almost unbearable. I grip the shaft of his cock and pull it out into the cool office air. It is long and hard and lean, as is the rest of him – perfect.

Leaning back onto the desk, my hand continues to hold on to him – not wanting to let him go even for a second. I can feel him growing amidst my fingers, and it makes me feel almost victorious. My legs wrap tightly around him, and it causes my skirt to slide up the rest of the way.

His lips continue to devour mine, and I can't help but take his face between my hands again and push his lips harder against mine – his kisses are Heaven. As he slips about between my wet thighs, I can feel him teasing me – his flesh gyrating against my moistness, but not entering me. I have wanted this man for what feels like for ever, and would accept any sweet torture that he should want to inflict! More unbearable with each brush of his sex against mine, I practically paw at him, needing to bring him even closer to me.

Our tongues dance together as I work away at his shirt buttons, quickly exposing his hairy chest – anxious to feel more of his skin on mine. 'Do you know how long I have wanted this?' I say, breathlessly, into his ear.

He just smiles and I melt. It is then, while I am lost in his beautiful smile, that he pushes his long cock into me. With one deep thrust, I am overcome with feelings both emotional and physical that I had never even dreamed possible. Our bodies feel to be a perfect fit as he slowly moves in and out of my wetness. Our faces close together and our chests are only separated by warm dew – I can feel every inch of him.

The quiet office fills with the smell of our hot, damp skin and my soft vanilla perfume. Breaking the silence is only the sound of him slipping in and out of me, and our faint moans. My insides grip his manhood tighter and my body trembles. I can literally feel my juices seeping out of me!

Pleasure shoots out of every bit of me and he leans forward, kissing me passionately as I climax.

Each shudder of my insides pushes him closer to his crisis, until finally taking him over the edge. I can feel my being quiver as he pulsates inside me, filling me with his warm milk. He cries out in ecstasy and it is like music to my ears. For so long I have wanted this – to be able to shake his hard, intimidating exterior, breaking it down with my desire for him. 'Edward. Oh, Edward…'

I say his name out loud as I break from my trance-like state and back to reality.

I am lying in my bed – alone. It is my bedroom that is filled with the smell of my vanilla perfume and my own sex, and my fingers are still moist from touching myself.

I close my eyes and say his name out loud again to make the fantasy seem just a bit more real. I say his name out loud to make him feel closer to me. I say his name out loud because for now, it's all I can do.

Choices
by Kate Franklin

I drift out of sleep into a sultry afternoon and stretch my limbs, thinking of my man. I know he should be home and I can already imagine his lean hard body pressed against mine.

With limbs still heavy from sleep, I get out of bed and pad barefoot to the window, feeling the mellow warmth of the bare floorboards beneath my feet. Parting the curtains a little, I open the window wide, breathing in the scent of the musky scented shrub clambering up the wall outside. A large bee enters its milky-pale blossoms, probing its fertile depths. Bright ribbons of sunlight penetrate the gaps in the curtains, striping my bare breasts with heat. Closing my eyes, I run my hands down over my stomach, feeling a different heat.

His footfall is soft and I don't hear him come in. 'Hey,' his familiar warm voice is low. 'How was the night shift? Is my nurse ready for a cup of tea?'

His dark eyes fall to my hands spread low on my stomach and he moves knowingly towards me with that animal-like grace he's blessed with. Pressing one big hand over mine, he pushes downwards, moistening our fingers. His hand works expertly on me as he kisses me. I have to pull the waistband of his shorts out carefully to release him, he's so steely hard. He pushes himself between my thighs, but doesn't enter. The heat between my legs turns to fire and I put my hand under his penis, bearing down on it, moving in a lazy rhythm. Then I'm coming, feeling like I always do that there's nothing better in the world, wanting to scream out at the pure ecstasy of it, as it goes on and on. As my orgasm fades away, he pulls himself from between my legs, spurting liquid warmth over my stomach.

I wait for him to quieten, then cream the sticky mound of my stomach against his flat one.

'Dirty bitch.'

'Now I'll have that tea. Then you can really fuck me.'

'Insatiable.'

I lie back on the bed sighing in deep contentment and my mind drifts back to when it all began…

In what now seems like another lifetime, I worked in an office. It was there I met Oliver, an arousing compensation for the grinding routine of my days. The attraction between us was instant and electric. I used to watch his long-fingered hands and imagine them all over me. His favourite trick was to come up silently behind me with that light, fluid tread of his and blow softly on the back of my neck, then knead my shoulders. He was sublimely intelligent, tall and lean, with fine, floppy black hair that fell over his high forehead and dark expressive eyes that smouldered whenever they looked my way.

But he was already in a relationship, and not wanting to be just another file in his in-tray, I reluctantly kept him at arm's length. When he left to start his own company, it was almost a relief. But I never forgot him.

The years wore on. I abandoned office life, entered nursing, married the wrong man and divorced –

heartbreakingly – but I was pretty much over it by that balmy day in late summer that was destined to shape my future. I was sitting outside a little French café on the edge of town waiting for a friend, when she rang me on my mobile to say she couldn't make it. Disappointed, I was about to leave when I felt a breath soft as cobwebs on the back of my neck. I spun round and, incredibly, there was Oliver. My knees went weak and I was back down the years in that dreary office, melting beneath his gaze.

He placed his hands on my shoulders and kissed me on both cheeks, smelling subtly of expensive aftershave. Looking sexy and stylish in an immaculately cut dark suit, his voice was still that low, rich one I remembered, 'How are you?'

My answer was from the heart, and even in only those bare moments, already from somewhere lower. 'Better for seeing you.'

His gaze smouldered and I could feel the old chemistry flare, working its way upwards until I could feel it in my cheeks, where I hoped I was glowing becomingly.

'Shall we?' Oliver indicated an empty table and we sat down. He ordered some coffees and removed his jacket, revealing the same broad shoulders and narrow waist my eyes used to linger greedily over. As he loosened his tie, I watched his hands, intently I guess, because he asked, '*What?*'

I had a sudden feeling for seizing the moment or it might be gone forever. 'I was just remembering how I used to imagine your hands all over me.'

He didn't bat an eyelid, as if it was no more than could be expected, grinning. 'And I couldn't look at you without getting an erection.'

I thought his grin was too smug, so with a quick glance around, slid my hand beneath the table. 'Nothing changed there then.'

'Christ, Hannah!'

His grin collapsed, and although I'm not usually the giggling sort, I couldn't help but do just that, he looked so twitchy. My hand squeezed his cock. 'It's okay, nobody's looking.'

'You'll get us thrown out.'

His embarrassment didn't stop his crotch from thrusting upwards though, and I kept my hand there, seizing the moment again. '*Hmmm*, maybe.'

His voice was husky, 'Are you free this afternoon?'

I nodded, trying not to look as ecstatic as a child surrounded by a pile of presents. 'I've been let down by the friend I was meeting.'

'Boyfriend?'

Our coffees arrived and I removed my hand, putting my elbows on the table, cupping my chin in my hands, relishing the look of him. 'No, girlfriend. So are you free too?'

'For you, yes.'

I've always been an outdoor girl. 'There's a lovely forest walk close by if that smart suit can cope.'

'No worries.'

I excused myself to go to the loo. When I returned, my pants were in my bag. Oliver pointed to where a multi-storey car park reared its ugly head behind the Georgian rooftops. 'I'm parked over there, or did you want to take your car?'

'No, I live near, so I walked in.'

Twenty minutes later we'd stuttered through the town's relentless traffic and were bowling along a thin grey ribbon of road. The short journey seemed endless, but at last the sign for the forest appeared and Oliver swung the low black convertible off the road, parking beneath a lofty stand of pines. Leaving the car, we took the wide grassy ride that snaked away before us, he pulling off his tie and undoing the top buttons of his shirt as we walked. Quite soon I spotted the trail I was looking for.

'This way.' I plunged between tall waving grasses, praying nature hadn't been too rampant since my last visit, seeking the secluded clearing I first discovered while out walking with my then husband, Ben. I'd tried to tempt him with some outdoor loving – blanket on the ground and all that stuff – but he was never one to bare his buttocks to the sky.

'Just where are you taking me?'

'Be patient, I'm looking for signs. I didn't get my orienteering badge in the Girl Guides for nothing…there's an old fallen tree…*look*, *there it is*. Only a bit further…*YES,* we're there.'

I squeezed through a gap in a tangle of tall overgrown bushes.

'Christ, woman, this had better be worth it.'

I breathed a sigh of relief, for the clearing was little changed, its floor carpeted with mossy grass and today, dappled with shifting sunlight.

Oliver emerged behind me, staring around at our camouflaged hideaway. '*Wow.*'

He dragged me over to a tree and leaned back against its ivy-clad trunk. 'Come here.' He pulled me against him. 'Before we go any further – as I'm feeling my behaviour's been rather mercenary, and okay I know you feel the same – but can I just say it's lovely to see you again.'

'Me too.' But really, *lovely* was far too *tea at the vicarage* for how I was feeling.

Breathing fast, Oliver deftly undid my silky dress and let it slip to the ground, while I pulled impatiently at his belt and zip, releasing his swollen penis, rubbing it against my belly. With a moan that said he didn't want to wait, he gripped my buttocks, bending his knees and lifting me off my feet. I was already so wet, he slid silkily inside me.

'Fucking hell, Hannah…can't wait…'

'Jesus, me neither.'

He thrust in short rapid movements, but I think if he'd simply remained still, the white heat would still have ripped through me. I buried my head in his chest to stifle my cries, but he moaned like a man in pain and must have frightened the wildlife.

He lowered me slowly to the ground, his softening penis sliding out, its wetness mingling with the sweat that had bloomed like mist on my belly. He took a deep trembling breath. '*Holy shite,* I haven't come so quick in years.'

'Bloody hell, me neither.'

We lay down on the spongy, dry grass then, limbs still quivering, my head resting on his stomach, we caught up with the years.

'I've got an expansion plan which means I'll be based here in the city. I've just bought a place down here,' he told me.

'*Really?*' Did dreams come true? If he answered my next question as I hoped, they might, 'Marriage?'

'Nearly; she had a lucky escape. Why're you grinning? You look like the cat that got the cream. Hey…' He pulled me up into his arms. 'It was always going to be good, wasn't it? Me and you. We have to see each other again…however, I do have a question first.'

'What?'

'Doesn't your pussy get cold without knickers?'

94

I saw him the very next evening. We'd intended going to a restaurant.

'Are you very hungry?' he asked when he arrived on my doorstep.

'Ravenous.'

He looked disappointed.

'For you.'

We undressed each other slowly in light dimmed to a rosy glow through closed red shutters. Men have never been beautiful to me, but Oliver was. He was smoothly toned with nothing over-muscular about him; even his penis in its flaccid state – long and slim – complimented his lean physique. But now it was stirring, and my heart began beating hard at its impressive transformation. Moving my hand up and down its rubbery length, I kissed my way down over his neck and hairless chest. Gripping his narrow hips, I crouched before his long flanks and taut belly, moving up and down so his hardness slid between my breasts. Kneeling, I took him into my mouth, but, already aching to have him inside me, I pushed my hand between my moistened thighs to ease the throbbing there. Oliver's breathing quickened, each outward breath a gasping moan, and his juices tasted sharp on my tongue. Then abruptly he pulled himself free and knelt down before me.

'I thought you liked it,' I whispered between rough kisses, greedily pushing his cock between my legs, and I could have yelled in frustration when he drew back.

'I've only been here minutes. I need to prove myself after peaking so early yesterday.'

He stretched out on the soft rug and I straddled his belly, pressing wetness over the dark arrow of hair there, feeling his erection taunting like a hard rod up over my back. It was no good. 'Too much foreplay,' I groaned, a desperate need pulsing through me. I knelt up, lowering myself onto him, leaning over him, pinning him to the ground by his arms. He closed his eyes, arching his head back. '*Ahhhh...I give in.*'

His fingers dug into my flesh and I rode him hungrily, drenching his groin. His voice was a whimper, 'Christ, I'm aching...'

When he came it was in a way too intense for sound, giving silent shuddering thrusts as my own peaks of rapture overwhelmed me.

Our loving from then on never lost its first promise. Lust grew into an intoxicating love, and when we could no longer bear to say goodnight, I sold my house and moved into Oliver's rambling old cottage on the heath. It was bliss, and also, let's be honest, being able to indulge my caviar taste after living on a meat paste budget wasn't a hardship.

I suppose nothing remains the same forever. Insidiously, Oliver's work began to overshadow our relationship. Once we'd made love as soon as he came in the door, often never getting beyond the stairs, now it was quickies grabbed here and there. Desperate to regain our old closeness, not to say lust, I booked a surprise holiday for us to a favourite Greek island of mine, but his reaction made me realize how little I really knew him. His eyes grew ice cold and his stark rejection had the impact of a physical blow, 'This deal I've been telling you about. Haven't you been listening? Of course I can't go. Go on your own.'

In the wintry silence of the next few days, I tried to convince myself it was only a row, but deep down I knew it was more fundamental than that. The ruthlessness that had made him such a successful businessman had spilled over into our lives. I've always been good at snap decisions, so after ringing a girlfriend and begging a bed, I packed a couple of suitcases, wrote Oliver a note, and left.

All week I didn't respond to his messages on my mobile, because none were apologetic. Oh I longed to speak to him, ached to hold him, but the holiday was looming uncancelled and, towards the end of that interminable week, I decided to go alone.

Chugging on the old ferry towards the island, jutting fingers of land beckoning inwards to white sheltered coves and verdant hillsides spiked with elegant cypresses, I wondered if I'd made the right decision. Alighting on the quayside, with the sun baking the whitewashed tranquillity of the harbour, I was greeted warmly by Aglaia, the holiday rep. She indicated a strongly-built, smiling man around my own age. '…and this is Nikos.' I looked up into a pair of mischievous dark eyes with golden lights and impossibly long black lashes. 'His parents own your apartment. He'll drive you there.'

'yia sou,' Nikos said. 'Ti kanete?'

'yia sou. I'm good, thank you.' I felt glad he'd chosen a few Greek words I knew, because he looked pleased.

A few days later, my skin was turning a light, toasty brown and my auburn hair was tinted with pale copper lights. I strolled in the olive groves, swam from white pebbled beaches, ate at friendly harbourside tavernas, and although Oliver still filled my waking thoughts, he no longer haunted my dreams.

Nikos often lingered for a chat in his popular family taverna. Apart from possessing arresting good looks, he had an easy, laughing way with him that, after Oliver's intensity, I found refreshing and totally disarming. Some parting advice from my girlfriend kept returning to me, making me smile – *the best way to get over one man is to get under another one.*

'Don't you get bored here?' I asked Nikos one evening.

'When a beautiful girl sit before me? *No*. Anyway, I am not here all year. I am a student, studying business.'

He laughed at my look of surprise. 'You think I am old for a student. Thirty-one is not so old. I shall work on the mainland when I get my degree.' He waved a hand around the busy taverna. 'Running this is no longer for me.' He inclined his head to one side. 'And you? Why all alone?'

I'd had a few glasses of wine and my barriers were down. 'Problems with my man.'

He leaned over and kissed my cheek in a sweet gesture. 'Your heart will mend.'

The following day, feeling adventurous, I hired a gaily-coloured boat from Nikos's grizzled father, Theodore, who was as old Greek as any you would find. With glaring chauvinistic reluctance to trust an inferior female with his craft, he demonstrated its outboard motor and how to pull in the anchor rope, grumbling, '*MAN* do motor, woman do *rope*.'

Luckily, the sea was calm that day, as I couldn't quite see myself coping with Theodore's small boat slicing through surf, and after passing four already claimed coves, I found the deserted one I was hoping for. After a bungled landing that would have had Theodore throwing his hands up in dismay, I moored his boat, scrambled gracelessly out onto warm shingle, laid out my towel and stripped to a floppy hat. Placing a parasol seaward for modesty, I drank too much wine after an olives and cheese lunch, then to the tinkle of goat bells from the cliff top high above, drifted off into velvety sleep.

The sun was low in the sky when I awoke, gazing drowsily around. Down by the water's edge, my parasol lay upended, blown there by the lively wind. I stood and raised my hands above my head, stretching. Then I froze, for watching me, from a boat that rose and fell gently on the shallow waves, was Nikos.

I sucked in a sharp breath as he slid from the boat and waded in, his olive-bronze skin glistening as the water ran down over his white shorts, the wet material moulding itself around blatant masculinity.

I didn't move, except to drop my arms, as he came to stand before me. Playfully, he removed my hat and tossed it on the shingle. 'You are overdressed. Come.' He caught my hand and ran with me towards a huddle of rocks beneath the cliffs, grabbing my towel on the way and laying it behind them. With his gaze locked on mine, he boldly stepped out of his shorts.

It was cheeky, but in that shimmering turquoise and golden world of sea and sun, it simply felt seductive, and I was already excusing myself with the thought, *you asked for this, Oliver.*

I cupped the pliant drop of Nikos's testicles in my hand, kneading them gently. 'I guess dropping one's shorts before a lady is the Greek version of foreplay?'

He grinned. 'You don't like?'

I didn't answer because I was having difficulty catching my breath as his long shaft lost its flaccidity and rose towards his flat belly. His voice was soft, 'Lie with me.'

We lay down on the towel, fastened together, a rock pressing into my bottom. Passion hadn't quite captured me at that point and a thought made me chuckle.

Nikos looked offended. 'I do something funny?'

'I'm between a rock and a hard place.'

He looked bemused, so I grasped the hard place. 'I'll explain later. Old English saying.'

He made love to me languidly at first, slow and teasing, entering me briefly, then pulling back, kissing down over my stomach, licking between my thighs, flicking and probing with his tongue as my hips arched upwards, wanting more. When at last he entered me, I was so utterly aroused, the beat of my orgasm began instantly and he thrust violently with an animal instinct as his cries mingled with my own.

We spent the rest of my holiday together making love, getting to know one another, making love again. During the evening I would sit in his family taverna in the angelica-scented air, content to watch him working, knowing he would soon be filling my bed.

On my last day, he took me to his friend's secluded villa above shady olive groves that plunged to the sea. 'My friend is away and I keep eye on things.'

After a cool drink, we went through to the airy bedroom where Nikos threw open blue french doors on to a wide ochre-tinted terrace dripping with crimson bougainvillea. We peeled off our clothes, and, cooled by a soft aromatic breeze, lay down on the bed, happy to just kiss for a long while. Nikos was a great one for simple loving, not just sex, and he loved to stroke my body, leaning back to study me, then pushing my hair back, fanning it out on the pillow, gazing at my face. I had already learned too he was an inventive lover and this time his fingers dipped into the wetness already soaking me and probed backwards.

When I was eighteen, I had an earthy boyfriend called Sean. I was unaware then that sex could be anything but dead straight, so when one night he pushed a finger between the cheeks of my bottom, I froze and indignantly asked him what he thought he was doing.

'Going where the sun don't shine, sweetheart.'

So believing you shouldn't knock anything until you've tried it, I let Sean go there and I was stunned at the depth of my orgasm, and now it was the same with Nikos. The world exploded and when my cries died to a whimper he knelt up, masturbating and ejaculating milkily over my sweat-dampened thighs.

'Naughty girl,' he scolded when we had our breath back. 'You will frighten the goats.'

The laughter suddenly died in his eyes and he gathered me quietly and tenderly into his arms. 'I am so sad at you leaving.'

I thought how at the beginning I'd ruthlessly used him as an antidote to Oliver (so shallow) and a voice in my head taunted back at me, *serve you right if you're just another Shirley Valentine. He's probably already thinking of his next conquest.*

I tried to joke to hide a pain that had started around my heart. 'Will you miss me? I know what you'll miss.' I let my hand travel downwards over his flat belly, but he gripped it, looking deep into my eyes.

'I think I fall in love.'

'*Oh, Nikos*...that's so...'

'*Shhh.*' He pressed a finger to my lips. 'So now we will say goodbye beautifully, like this...' He lay on top of me, his flaccid penis between my thighs, kissing me deeply. 'And this...' As he began to harden, he pushed himself inside me and I felt full of him as he grew. We hardly moved, holding each other's gaze, and when we came, it was together, looking into each other's eyes. It wasn't fucking; it was truly making love.

Afterwards, we stood on the terrace watching an enormous sun go down in a fiery blaze on the horizon, not talking, and I wished at that moment I could stay there forever, leaning back against Nikos, his arms drawn around me.

I left the island the next morning beneath a pink dawn, with Nikos' waving figure a dwindling speck on the quayside, and that pain that had begun around my heart was almost unbearable. I thought of Oliver. Was it possible to love two men at once?

That evening, travel weary but clear-headed, I faced Oliver and knew the words I'd planned on the journey home would hold good.

All that is now two years ago. My tea arrives and I look up and think how much I adore this husband of mine as he enters our bedroom.

'I've just been thinking about the first time you made love to me.'

'With the sky our witness.'

He stretches out on the bed beside me.

'We'll let the tea brew.'

His hand strokes the still small swell of my stomach. 'We must think of names.'

'If it's a boy, I'd like to name him after his father.'

He thinks for a minute then nods in satisfaction. 'Yes, I like. Nikos he will be.'

Flash Flood
by Lynn Lake

When my boyfriend, Donny, broke his leg tube-tobogganing with a bunch of his drunken buddies two days before we were scheduled to jet off to Australia for Christmas vacation, I was thoroughly p.o.'d. I thought about cancelling the trip, staying home on the farm outside snowy Grand Prairie, Alberta. But since the hotel reservation was non-refundable, and the local seven-day forecast called for bitter cold followed by brutal cold, I didn't think about it for too long. I kissed Donny and his cast goodbye and waded through the snowdrifts to my waiting taxi.

Living in the rural area with my parents, the farthest I'd ever been away from home before was Edmonton, for a family funeral. The down-under wonder trip represented my first chance to get out on my own, spread my wings, expand my horizons, see new things and meet new people before my twenty-first birthday. Being a country girl, I'd toppled a few cows and flashed a few truck drivers in my time, but that's about as wild as it'd ever gotten for me.

It was -30 C when I stepped on the plane in Edmonton, + 30 C when I skipped off in Sydney. I dashed out of the

103

airport and into Old Sol's smiling embrace, hurling my toque in the air like a sun-struck Mary Tyler Moore.

Sydney was spectacular: the Opera House, the Harbour Bridge, the 'Rocks', hot golden-sand beaches and warm crystal-clear ocean. I got all the formal touristy things out of the way early, so I had something to postcard my parents, and Donny. Then I tied on a string bikini and dove onto the beach, pale winter homebody browning ripe and juicy under the blazing sun.

Usually, after a tough day at the beach, I'd catch a quick catnap in my hotel room before going out for dinner, enjoying the Sydney nightlife. But when I'd spent one particular eye-opening afternoon basking on Cobbler's Beach, a nude beach, I found myself fired up by more than hot sun and twinkling seascape.

I sat on the edge of my bed in my tenth floor hotel room, glowing. My mind floated back to one particularly handsome couple I'd scoped: a rugged, blonde All-Australian hunk and his big-boobed, sandy-haired girlfriend. They'd been frolicking surfside, naked-as-you-please, hard bodies gleaming bronze, soft body parts jiggling and bobbing delightfully.

I slid off the bed and stood in front of the mirror on the wall, hands dangling at my sides like a sexual gunslinger, prickly-itchy for action. I was wearing just a white 'Aussie Rules' t-shirt and pale blue shorty-shorts, and I stared at myself, nipples hardening and pussy dampening, as I pictured the blonde beach couple (Guy and Kylie, as I'd named them) coming together in the water, nude, sun-browned bodies melding together, lips meeting in a love embrace.

Guy crushed Kylie against his muscled chest, his big hands splaying over her arched back, down her back, onto her plush, rounded bottom. He gripped and squeezed her taut, golden butt cheeks, Kylie moaning into his mouth, their pink tongues flashing together in the brilliant sunshine.

We had the glittering beach all to ourselves, Guy and Kylie in the surging water, kissing and frenching and fondling, me on-shore, stripping away my bikini, flashing the lovers and the continent. They glanced at me, their eyes shining, appraising my bared body and nodding their approval. Then Kylie tilted her head back, blonde hair streaming, and Guy attacked her throat, kissing and licking the soft, vulnerable skin, biting.

I gasped as Kylie gasped, staring at my wicked reflection, my shirt and shorts somehow puddled at my feet. I lifted my hands, fingers trembling, and cupped my naked breasts. 'Yes!' I groaned, squeezing the electrified, handful mounds, sending current sparking all through me.

I shook out my long, black tresses and kneaded my tan-lined boobs, pink nipples jutting rigid, sniffing the salty air, buzzing with anticipation. The Aussies were kissing each other again, Guy's strong hands plying Kylie's plump buttocks, Kylie grabbing Guy's head and savaging his mouth.

I inched twitching fingers up to my straining nipples, my whole body shaking, heavy with erotic heat. And then…rain hissed down.

I was standing in front of the open sliding door that led out to the balcony, just a thin, gauze curtain separating me from the outside world, and I briefly watched the raindrops peck into the green indoor-outdoor carpeting. But I wasn't about to let a little rain ruin my illusion; I incorporated it into my fantasy.

I stepped closer to the opening, still reflected in the mirror, my mind's eye still on Guy and Kylie. I stuck my hand out the curtain and grabbed some liquid sunshine, splashed it over my body. I swear I could hear it sizzle. I splashed on some more, until I was almost as wet as the daring, dazzling couple making love in the ocean. Then I placed my damp hands back on my damp, tingling breasts and squeezed again, crawling my fingers up and pinching my needful nipples.

'Yes!' I moaned, a sweet burning sensation shimmering in from my buds all through my body. I gently pulled on my engorged nipples, then not so gently.

I closed my eyes and was swept away, Guy gripping his long, hard cock and plunging it into Kylie's pussy. She cried out, jumping up and wrapping her gleaming legs around Guy's waist, her arms around his neck. He held her by the bum and pumped his hips, cock gliding back and forth in her stretched-out pussy, right in front of little overexposed me.

I slid a hand down my stomach and in between my legs, feeling the soft, springy fur there, then pressing into my puffed-up clit. My head spun and I shuddered, pussy flaming wet-hot as the rest of me.

Guy pistoned his glistening cock in Kylie's gripping pussy, muscles standing out in stark, mouth-watering relief on his legs and arms and back. Kylie held on to the man's neck, bouncing her bum on his thrusting pole, swarming her tongue into his mouth, her body and breasts rocking in rhythm to Guy's pounding cock.

I anxiously kneaded my soft, sensitive tit-flesh, rubbing and rubbing and rubbing my button. I thrust a hand out the curtain and scooped up more rainwater, flinging it on my pussy and chest, oiling my erotic actions. I pinched a nipple so hard I thought it would burst, me along with it.

The rain was pouring down now, inches away from me, dark clouds rolling in and swallowing the sun. But all I saw was Guy in the sparkling water under the cloudless

106

sky, fucking Kylie. She spasmed in his muscular arms, breasts shuddering, body jolted by ecstasy. She clutched the man's face to her tits as orgasm broke loose inside her and washed her away.

I dove three fingers into my slippery folds, plunging two knuckles deep. I pumped my pussy like Guy was pumping the orgasm-blissed Kylie, thumb riding my clit, fingers rolling my nipples. Guy's mouth broke open and his body jerked. He pulsed hot, salty semen deep into Kylie, the two of them coming as one, shaking so badly they threatened to topple over and tumble into the ocean.

And right then, a wet, wicked orgasm welled up from my finger-churned pussy and thumb-buffed clit and went tidal-waving through my water-dappled body, sending me out to sea with my fantasy lovers. My knees buckled under the wall of ecstasy, and I squirted my joy, sinking to the sand/carpet and gasping for air.

It was a full minute before I finally reopened my eyes. I blinked at the nude, kneeling girl in the mirror. Then I eased drenched fingers out of my sopping pussy, vaguely wondering if the puddle on the carpet would leave a stain. Still dripping, I climbed to my feet and staggered through the curtain out onto the balcony, letting the driving rain cool me down a little, wash away the sticky evidence of my self-fulfilment.

The spray felt good on my superheated skin, and I arched my body to meet it, tilting my head back and closing my eyes and opening my mouth. It was a full-fledged rainstorm now, lightning streaking the blackened sky, thunder booming, flash flooding likely in some of the outlying areas, I knew from the literature. But I was way ahead of the game – flashing after flooding my room.

Someone giggled.

My eyes flew open and I straightened up with a snap. Standing on the balcony next to mine, close by the railing less than six feet away, were a man and a woman, staring at me, lascivious smiles lighting up their faces, and my naked body.

I flung an arm over my breasts, a hand in between my legs. The man laughed, said something in German or Dutch, and I shrieked, 'I'm Canadian!'

He pointed at his eyes, then into my room. 'We see,' he said, grinning.

I spun around. The mirror in my room was clearly visible through the gauze curtain. I spun back around, my hand jumping from my butt back to my pussy. The man and the woman were as soaked as I was, and standing at the angle they were…they'd been watching me get off in the mirror!

'We see,' the man confirmed, teeth gleaming.

I blushed red as Ayers Rock.

'I'm Ralf,' the guy said pleasantly, like witnessing a girl pleasuring herself was all in a day's vacation. He held his companion's shoulders. 'And this is Astrid. We…join you?'

My mouth clanged open as I watched Ralf climb over his balcony and onto mine. He helped Astrid on over, and we all stood there together on the forty-square-feet of carpet and concrete and railing, me naked as the break of day. My guests soon joined me in that, as well.

They quickly and unabashedly peeled off their soaking duds, stepping out of the sodden piles of clothing as blazingly, blatantly nude as I was – right out there on my ocean-view perch for all commercial and recreational vessels, parasailers and pilots, and neighbouring balcony-dwellers to see. I could hardly believe what was happening, what my inadvertently public exhibition of lust had gotten me into.

I stared at the pair, the sky dousing us with rain. They looked like twins – both tall and lean, with sun-bleached blonde hair and eyebrows, all-over tans, and big, blue, expressive eyes. Astrid's hair was braided into twin ponytails, her breasts high, almost upturned, protruding, creamed-coffee nipples punctured by twin silver barbells. Her pussy was bare as the Australian outback, a silver ring through her puffy lips.

Ralf's face was squarer than Astrid's, his hair buzzcut at the sides, his body smooth and sinewy, tattoos adorning his shoulders. My eyes drifted lower, down to his cock, widening even further when I saw that the thick, tan-coloured member was growing, rising up right before my very, innocent eyes.

Ralf pointed at the mirror and said, 'We help you enjoy…' He made a circling motion with his finger. 'All of us.'

Astrid nodded, smiling. She touched my shoulder, and I shivered. Despite the warm rain and sultry temperature. Then she strolled in behind me and gripped my shoulders, squeezed them, pressing her breasts and body against my back. A sensual lightning bolt shot through me, shimmering at the pointed tips of my breasts and deep in my pussy.

I felt weak and safe and wonderful, Astrid holding me against her soft, hot body, rain spraying my tingling skin. I closed my eyes and sighed. Then I felt hands on my boobs, and my eyes flew open. Ralf was cupping my breasts, caressing them, staring at me with his bright, blue eyes. His long fingers captured the swollen peaks of my tits and pinched.

'Mmmm!' I moaned.

It was pure insanity, getting felt up by a couple of complete strangers on an over-exposed hotel balcony in the middle of a thunderstorm. But my uptight upbringing and safety-first attitude were stowed nine thousand miles away. And so when Ralf softly kissed me, I leaned into his lips, drawn like lightning to an iron rod.

He kissed Astrid over my shoulder, then me again, more firmly this time. And when he came back a third time, we mashed our mouths together. He darted his tongue in between my lips, bumping into my tongue, his cock pressing hard and hot against my belly.

We swirled our tongues together, my head spinning in time, Ralf moving his hips, sliding his prick against my slick skin. Then he pulled back and frenched with Astrid, and another set of hands grasped my breasts – Astrid's. She cupped and massaged my boobs, never breaking tongue-contact with Ralf.

Ralf put his hands on my hips and lowered his head, tickling one of my stiffened nipples with the tip of his tongue. I gasped. Astrid bit into my neck, clutching my tits, feeding them to her lover – my lover.

Ralf swirled his wet, pink tongue around first one engorged bud and then the other, painting my pebbly aureoles. I quivered with delight, Astrid licking and kissing and biting my neck, squeezing my breasts, Ralf tonguing my nipples, the three of us hanging out there for the whole wide rain-drenched world to see.

Ralf sealed his lips around one of my nipples and sucked on it, and I went wetter yet. He tugged my charged-up bud even harder and higher, his hot breath flooding my chest. Then he disgorged my nipple, inflamed and dripping, and sucked on my other bud. Astrid's nimble fingers took up where the guy's mouth left off, rolling my nipple. And when she bit into my earlobe at the

110

same time Ralf bit into an aching nipple, I yelped with joy, overcome by it all.

It went on and on like that, my brain gone fuzzy and my body limp and languid, overheated. Until at last I found myself on my knees on the sopping carpet, Astrid next to me, Ralf's big, dripping cock between the two of us. Lightning lit up the sky, thunder rattling the building, as Astrid encircled Ralf's jumping shaft with her fingers and pulled him into her mouth, sucked on his hood. Her blazing blue eyes locked onto mine, daring me to do the same.

Ralf groaned. I looked up at the trembling man, rain streaming down his sun-browned torso. I held onto his leg for support, my hand travelling over a firm, clenched buttock. Then I felt something bump against my cheek, and I looked back down. It was Ralf's cock, shiny from Astrid's mouth, ready for mine.

I swallowed, hard. Then I opened my mouth and took Ralf's hood in between my lips. He groaned, grabbed onto my head. I brushed Astrid's hand away and gripped the man's shaft, growing bold and wicked as the piled-up black clouds overhead.

Ralf's cock throbbed in my hand. I pushed my dizzy head forward, taking more and more of him into my mouth, before pulling back, sucking on his cock. I bobbed my head up and down, pulsing meat sliding between my lips. I grasped his tightened sack, and his cock jerked in my mouth.

The feeling of wanton power from having a man by the cock and balls was electrifying, and I was loath to relinquish it. But Astrid wrestled Ralf's prick away from me and sucked on it herself. We passed the waterlogged dong back and forth between the two of us, licking and

111

sucking, diving down and then slow-pulling back up, again and again, the heavens pouring down upon us.

Then Astrid slid her lips along one side of Ralf's pulsating erection, and I the other, sharing the man. He clawed at our hair, his body vibrating. We swept back and forth on his shaft, our tongues meeting on the veiny underside, our lips meeting at the mushroomed tip. Ralf pushed our heads together, and we girls kissed, frenched, tongues excitedly entwining.

Eventually, I ended up on all-fours, with Ralf behind me and Astrid sprawled out and spread wide in front of me. She gripped her tits and looked meaningfully at her baby-faced snatch, then at me. I gulped, grabbed onto the woman's thighs and dipped my tongue into her glistening petals.

She moaned as I wagged my tongue across her pussy lips, tasting and teasing, then dragged my tongue slow and heavy up her slit, from bumhole to silver-ringed clit hood. I licked her over and over, like I knew what I was doing, Ralf urging me on with cock-whacks to my trembling butt cheeks.

I spread Astrid's pussy open with my fingers and licked at her inner pink, toying with her silver ring, before latching my lips onto her swollen clit and sucking. Ralf rewarded me by pushing his cock into my pussy. He sank inside me like a beach umbrella into wet sand, until his body touched up against my butt. Then he started fucking me, holding my hips and stroking his cock in and out of my smouldering pussy.

I had trouble breathing, keeping a slippery grip on sanity and consciousness, as I sucked on a woman's clit while a man pumped cock into my pussy. Astrid pressed my head into her twat, the babe's musky scent and tangy juices flooding my senses, Ralf rocking me from behind,

112

filling me to overflowing, the rain sheeting down on our burning bodies and rising as steam.

Lightning crackled and thunder boomed, and I quivered out-of-control, a mammoth orgasm rising up from pussy and cascading through my body, sending me sailing. I desperately licked Astrid's slit, fingered her clit. She screamed and shuddered, hot, spicy juices pouring into my mouth, just about drowning me. Ralf cried out, too, splashing against me, warm semen flooding my gushing pussy, the three of us a roiling sea of ecstasy.

It took a long time for us to disentangle, everyone soaked and satisfied. Ralf helped Astrid and me to our feet, whereupon we all received a rousing ovation from the two guys hanging off the balcony directly above mine. They ended up figuring in my vacation plans, too, later that night.

It's amazing what a change of scenery and a little exposure will do for your outlook on life – and your sex life.

Well Suited
by Jordana Winters

'Damn. Now there's a man who can wear a suit,' she purred.

'Where?'

'Just walked in.'

In a semi-crowded upscale bistro, three pairs of eyes fixed on the door.

'Try not to be too obvious,' Brooke said to her friends in a hushed voice.

Brooke glanced at her two best friends. She was lucky to have them. She always looked forward to their weekly girls' date. It was their custom to go to the gym together and then grab coffee or food. Cheryl's husband looked after the kids while Kate's man did fuck knows what.

'Yeah. Good eye,' Cheryl said, and smiled coyly before returning her attention to her half-consumed strawberry tart.

'I do so love a hot man in a suit. Reminds me of that guy who was in the office of that last temp job I worked,' Brooke said, still eyeing the man at the counter.

'You never mentioned him,' Kate quizzed.

'He wasn't worth mentioning. He was married, had a couple of kids. I asked someone about him. Mostly he was eye candy. Must have known I was hot for him. He was an instructor or something. Had a classroom set up right across from the lunchroom? I always gave him the look when I went for coffee.'

'Brooke. You're such a tease,' Cheryl snorted as she drank her coffee.

'Not at all. I only ever said hi to him when we passed in the hall. It was him that spoke to me first. Did the good morning, how are you bit. He was into it. Whatever. I imagine he was flattered. He was in good shape. Sometimes saw him minus his jacket. Nice broad shoulders. Bald. Well groomed. Goatee. It was the suit though. He just looked so hot in that thing,' Brooke reminisced.

'You should make that your next conquest. A hot guy in a suit. How long has it been now?' Kate teased, knowing Brooke was in the middle of a sexual dry spot.

'Going on four months. This is the point where I start itching for it. That's a fine idea though. I have yet to fuck a 'business professional',' Brooke joked.

'Go for it and make sure to tell us all about it, especially the nasty details,' Cheryl said and laughed.

'You are the most sexually obsessed married woman I know,' Kate said to Cheryl.

'Billy's shift schedule changed. He's on nights. I'm at work all day. We barely cross paths. But, between now and Sunday,' she paused, 'my husband is going to fuck me!'

'Hallelujah. Never mind him fucking you. You fuck him,' Brooke joked.

Brooke eyed the back of the man on his way out the door, coffee in hand.

'Yeah. I bet he's got a great ass hidden under that suit.'

It was Wednesday. Hump day. Everything that could have gone wrong in her day had. She was looking forward to going home, eating yesterday's leftover Chinese food for dinner and sinking into a hot bath.

Upon getting into her car Brooke managed to get a ragged fingernail caught on the thigh of her stockings. She watched as the tear of the material continued upwards and stopped only because its path was blocked by black lace and elastic.

'Goddamnit!' she cursed.

That reminded her. She thought of her sock drawer and tried to recall if she had any packages of stockings left. Nope. She'd opened the last package this morning. An eight-dollar pair of stockings had at least managed to survive the day. What a fuckin' waste. On the bright side – at least the other leg was salvageable.

She considered wearing a pantsuit to her early morning meeting with the higher-ups of the company she worked for, but thought better of it. In a skirt Brooke would look her smartest – meaning she needed to pick up more stockings. There was a Macy's on the way home. That would do. She could be in and out in five minutes.

Walking through the store, she was a woman on a mission. Her high heels clicked noisily against the floor. The store was all but empty with a few customers and seemingly even fewer employees around.

With her purchase tucked away in her purse, she walked past the men's department and noticed a deliciously suited man milling through the clothes racks. She slowed her pace and cut into an aisle.

She took a better look at him as she slowly moved closer. He was wearing a dark suit with a blue shirt on underneath, although it wasn't tucked it. His tie had been loosened. Fuck. Brooke loved that casual look. He couldn't have been much older than her, late thirties maybe. He was very well groomed with a closely cropped haircut and tightly groomed goatee. She'd wager he had softer hands than most men and wore expensive cologne. She had to have him.

As if sensing he was being watched he looked up and his eyes connected with hers. Very nice. She didn't look away. She held his gaze as she walked towards him.

'Are you lost?' he asked, his voice deep and baritone.

'Lost?'

'I assume you aren't shopping for yourself,' he joked as she propped her arm up against a clothes rack.

She quickly glanced down at his left hand. No ring. Good.

'Maybe I'm shopping for a boyfriend...my father or brother,' she rebutted.

'I don't think so,' he replied, and stared at her knowingly.

'I was on my way home. Tore my stockings.'

She pulled up her skirt showing him the torn stocking.

'Oh dear. What a shame,' he said, not taking his eyes off her exposed thigh.

'That suit is really hot. Or...I should say – you are hot in that suit,' she said, her eyes fixed on his.

How ridiculous. She couldn't believe the words were coming out of her mouth. That was one hell of a pick-up line. She considered that if a man said those same words to a woman he was liable to be punched. How wonderful the things women could get away with.

She reached for a shirt hanging from a nearby rack.

'I think you'd look really good in this. Why don't you try it on for me?'

He didn't even blink. Did this type of thing happen to him often? She didn't care. She spun on her heel and walked towards the changing rooms.

'You're coming, I hope,' she said, not bothering to turn around.

Her eyes scanned the area. There wasn't a soul around. She walked to an empty changing room in the farthest corner. She turned and grabbed hold of his tie and pulled him in after her.

She dropped her purse, pulled off her coat and leaned against the wall.

'What's your name?' he asked.

'Kate,' she lied, thinking how much her friend would appreciate being directly involved in her latest sexual escapade.

'Richard.'

'Well Richard. I sure would like to see you minus that suit.'

She made no offer to help him undress. She had no intention of it. She watched intently as he slowly pulled off his tie and slid out of his shirt. His confidence was unfettered. Heat radiated from her sex upwards. The room suddenly felt like it was a thousand degrees.

He was in good shape. With his shirt off his skin was darker than it should be considering the season. He probably paid for an artificial suntan. His chest was wide and his arms strong.

Brooke undid the buttons of her blouse and let her suit jacket fall to the floor. They had yet to break eye contact as if they were in some sort of stare-off. Let him win. She averted her eyes to his crotch as he unbuttoned his pants. His hard-on was obvious. Looked like he had a good-sized cock. She guessed she wasn't going to be disappointed.

She reached down for her purse, found the inner pocket and the condom inside. She pulled it out and tossed it at him.

She tugged at the bottom of her skirt and pulled it up her thighs until it was tight around her hips. Looking him in the eye again she reached down and stroked herself through her panties, feeling the dampness of the material against her fingers.

'Very nice,' she purred at him.

She watched as he pulled his underwear and pants down and let them collect in a heap around his ankles. His cock jutted out in front of him as he fumbled with the condom wrapper.

She hooked her fingers through her panties, slid them down her thighs and kicked them off to rest at his feet. She rotated her hips seductively as her fingers slipped between her moist folds and traced over her clit.

'You going to fuck me, Richard?' she purred.

'Fuckin' right,' he growled, the former professional businessman persona having now disappeared.

She turned away from him and leaned against the wall, moving her right foot up to rest on a small bench.

She then felt his hot hands come to rest on her hips. His fingers roughly kneaded the skin of her ass before moving down to her pussy. She felt his fingertips trace over her clit before opening her up for his cock to follow.

Brooke moaned out an 'ugggghhh' as he forced himself into her. She winced in pleasure as his girth spread her open.

She braced her hand against the wall as her free hand slithered down her belly to play with her clit.

He grunted behind her as he roughly pounded into her. His hand reached around to her breasts which he grabbed at, pushing her bra up and leaving the under wire to pinch pleasantly into the skin above her breasts. He tweaked and squeezed her nipples.

'Fuck. That's nice,' she coaxed him on, lost in the feelings that were erupting in her cunt.

She didn't know how long he banged her for – it could have been five minutes, it could have been three. It didn't matter. It was quick and that's all she wanted. He fucked her relentlessly, hard and in a consistent rhythm. Now this was a man who knew how to fuck.

'Oh my…FUCK…' she squeaked out as she came, her legs shaking violently beneath her.

His orgasm was quick to follow hers. His fingers roughly squeezed at her hips and breasts. She would no doubt have some form of blood bruises tomorrow.

Brooke turned around to face him once he'd pulled away from her. She reached down for her panties and quickly stuffed them in her purse, at the same time fumbling with her buttons. She had her skirt pulled down and her jacket back on before he had pulled the condom off.

'Thanks. That was really…crazy,' she said, searching for an appropriate word and coming up empty.

She looked at herself in the mirror as she smoothed out her clothes and hair. Then, she moved towards him and kissed him hard and quick on the lips.

'I suppose asking for your number would be a waste of time,' he asked, clearly already knowing the answer but trying anyway.

'Yeah. Probably,' she replied, feeling very much like a wanton slut.

She reached for the door handle.

'Take it easy,' she said, walked out, through the men's department and out the door.

Scratch that one off her list. Finally she'd had her man in a suit.

Bananaz
by Dee Dawning

Exhausted after a hard day's work, I crash on the couch, hoping to take a well-deserved nap. As I start to doze off, my slumber is interrupted by voices – giggles actually – emanating from the kitchen. I recognize my live-in girlfriend Teri's voice, but I can't seem to place the others.

Curious, I decide to see what they are up to. Trying not to interrupt what they are doing, I stealthily rise from the couch and furtively inch toward the kitchen doorway. I haven't taken three steps when I hear someone gagging, accompanied by uproarious laughter. Then, the sensuous voice of my Teri says, 'Shelly, you need to open wide and relax. Do it slower. Don't be in such a hurry, watch me.' Now, my curiosity is piqued. What could she be talking about? Arriving at the kitchen portal, I surreptitiously sneak a peak around the corner.

Surprised, but pleased, I glimpse the forms of three lithe, bikini-clad, young women, standing around the table, watching Teri. Since my view of Teri is from behind, I am unable to ascertain what she is showing Shelly, whichever one she may be.

Wearing her skimpiest black micro-bikini, Teri's long blond hair is visible to me as is her hourglass figure and fine, shapely legs, which join at her remarkable derriere. Her head is thrown back slightly and I can see that one of her arms is performing something near her face. Since I cannot make out what Teri is up to, I study the other girls for clues. They are without exception lovely: a Hispanic raven-haired, dark-eyed beauty, a red head with a fair complexion, freckles and all (how I love redheads). and an African-American charmer, whom I recognise from Teri's practices. Having never met, I assume the other two are Teri's fellow dancers as well.

The black beauty, who stands almost directly opposite me locks eyes and smiles. What a fantastic smile, with perfect pearly white teeth contrasting her medium brown colouring. As her eyes fix on mine she tosses me a kiss with her lips, then lifts up a yellow object and inserts it into her mouth. I realize it is a banana. Still watching me with mischievous glee in her bright eyes, she shoves it in and out, stroking the remainder of the banana with her other hand.

I can feel my own personal banana begin to stir. I notice the other girls are also holding bananas. The redhead notices what black beauty is doing and follows her eyes to me. Throwing a hand up over her mouth she cannot stifle the laugh that escapes. Then the black-haired girl notices me, and smiles. Joel, the voyeur, has been discovered.

Teri spins around with a banana halfway down her throat and starts choking when she sees me. She jerks the banana out and grabbing my hand brings me into the kitchen, falling into my arms laughing.

'Looks like you caught us being wicked,' she laughs.

124

'Wicked.' I say, 'It looked more like you were starving. What's going on?'

'Joel, honey. These are my friends, Lisa, Shelly and Gloria. They work with me.' I nod. She goes on, 'We were sunning by the pool and somehow the subject of blow jobs came up and then it evolved to deep throating, so we came up here to see if we could do it.'

Gloria takes the banana out of her mouth. Eyeing my somewhat bulging crotch, she licks her lips and says, 'Pleased to eat you.'

Shelly is shocked. 'Glory, this is Teri's boyfriend.'

'Hey girl, don't I know it. Look at him. Check out his curly hair and friendly smile. Doesn't that just make you wanna plant a happy-face on him?'

Smacking her lips, and giving Gloria a high five, Lisa adds, 'You're there, Glory. He surely is a hunk. Look at those beautiful blues and check those muscles. What are you? Six-three, maybe two-twenty.'

'Six-two, two-ten and he belongs to moi,' says Teri, locking arms with me, reinforcing her claim.

Gloria chides Teri, 'Girl, why you sucking on bananaz when the top banana is at your fingertips. C'mon girl. Show us how you do it.'

By now, my zinger is at about two o'clock and rising. Teri looks at me and shrugs. 'I'm game if you are?'

Good question. I think. Game? I probably am game for a hot blowjob but am I game to have Teri deep throat me in front of her lovely cohorts? I'm shocked Teri is.

'I suppose I am, but I need to take a quick shower. I want to do it in bed and if I'm going to be naked so is everyone.'

Everyone eagerly says okay or nods in assent.

No sooner, do I get the words out and Gloria is out of her hot pink bikini. Gloria is glorious. Her fine mocha coloured tits with chocolate nipples reminds me of how much I love chocolate. Her legs, thin and shapely are magnificent specimens that support her tight round protruding ass. She is the whole package and she seems to know it.

As I head to the bathroom to take a shower, a bevy of beautiful women follow me, led by my very own, now naked, Teri. Like her friends, and most dancers, she is lean, with thin shapely legs, slim waist and shapely but moderate-sized breasts, with pert protruding nipples. What sets Teri apart from other modern women is she doesn't shave her pubis. She is a natural blond and her lightly trimmed, blond bush is a point of pride.

By now, Lisa is also naked. With her light brown skin, dancer's shape and deep brown eyes, I am enthralled. However, it is her unique pussy that I find most arousing. Her labia and her clitoris look like it is designed specifically for sex, extending almost an inch out beyond her vagina. It reminds me of a human Venus Fly Trap.

I undress for my shower, as eight prurient eyes study my every move. When I remove my briefs, the girls express a combination of catcalls and whistles. Gloria and Shelly grasp my penis for a short time. Unfortunately, Teri beats them off, before they manage to beat me off. Shelly says, 'Wow! How big is that? Do you think you can swallow all of that, Ter?'

'I can, if she can't.' Gloria brazenly declares.

Shelly, has now shed her teal blue bikini and I cannot decide which of these sexy wenches turns me on the most. They are all so beautiful and yet so divergent, like a cross-section of womanhood and right now, they all desire me. Shelly's skin is luminescent, almost white with a tiny hint of pink, interrupted by a flurry of friendly freckles on the top of her medium, upright breasts and shoulders. Her

126

perky pink nipples and red bearded mound above her pink vagina excite me. Like Teri, she declines to shave her pubis, which is flame red, like her hair.

Teri once again stakes her claim of ownership by stepping into the shower and washing me, especially my expanding erection. Lisa, Shelly and Glory peek around the shower curtain, cracking salacious remarks and reaching in. They admire my grand phallus as I emerge from the shower and Shelly announces, 'I think you should share Joel's penis with us to practice our deep throating.'

Lisa follows. 'Yes, it's only fair, Teri.'

As I listen to their protestations, I sense a weakening in Teri's resolve. Perhaps she is beginning to realize the torrent of desire that has been unleashed. She takes my hand, leads me to, and sets me down on, the edge of the bed. On her knees, she takes me in her beautiful mouth. The girls ooh and aw as they gather around observing the spectacle. They are impressed as Teri swallows my whole cock. She had done this before, so I knew she could. Teri is a talented as well as beautiful girl.

I notice the girls are masturbating, watching my cock delving deeply into Teri's oesophagus. Intrigued, Gloria wants to participate, but she doesn't know how. She descends to her knees beside Teri and begins to tease Teri's twat. Then she grabs the base of my cock and strokes it. Teri relinquishes my cock, saying 'Here. You want to suck it so bad. Be my guest.'

Glory fills the void. She is a very animated cocksucker, stroking my shaft in a twisting motion and revolving her head around the head, her tongue flittering across my sensitive frenulum. She even begins to hum. 'Ummmmmmm, ummmm.' The humming increases the stimulation to my cock.

The balmy aroma of aroused female sex organs (hot pussy) is prevalent, permeating my olfactory senses. I am getting so excited my heart begins to palpitate so I lay back and spread my arms hoping to calm down, but Lisa and Shelly view this as an opportunity.

Leaving Gloria, Teri jumps up on the bed. Gliding toward me, she straddles my face, snuggling her hot, wet, tasty snatch against my hungry mouth. I begin to satisfy her lust, tonguing and nibbling on her clitoris. I love the view from here, taking in the entire length of her sexy body, from her mound, to her belly, to her shapely breasts with her pretty face peeking down at me between her breasts.

I want to knead those breasts and tickle her nipples with my fingers but my hands are now occupied on other urgent business. Lisa and Shelly have nestled their love-nests against each of my hands and are manipulating each of them as if they were their personal sex toy. Shelly uses my left hand to wander through her pubic forest of red hair; using my fingers to massage her clit and pussy.

Lisa prefers a different technique of stimulation; her hand on top of mine, inserting multiple fingers into her remarkable cockpit with the protruding labia and clitoris. I can sense Lisa's other hand massaging her clitty. Lisa's love canal is fully enlarged and, to my surprise, after inserting four fingers, she manages, with considerable difficulty, to force my entire, rather large, fist into her expanded cavern.

'Rub my G spot she utters.' Repeating it several times. Having never before, had my entire hand within a woman's cunt, I wasn't sure what to do, but I aim to please. Feeling around with my fingers, I come across what must resemble (if one could view it) a tiny volcano, sans the lava. I rub the indentation with my forefinger and ask, 'Is that it?' I think she nods for I could feel the up and down motion clear down on my wrist, so I massage the indentation with my forefinger.

Since my face is buried in Teri's wet snatch, I can't see the recipients of my manual machinations, but I suspect Shelly and Lisa are also pleasuring each other.

Meanwhile, Glorious Gloria is doing an exemplary job of sucking my sizable rod, even though each time she tries to swallow my entire shaft, she gags. That's okay. I like her spunk (oops! wrong word) – enthusiasm. She can suck me off anytime she wants. As long as Teri lets her, that is. However, Glory finally notices that she's the only girl giving and all her friends are receiving. Deciding to debunk the myth that it's better to give than receive, she stops sucking and takes my cock out of her mouth. As occupied as I am, I barely notice but when I suddenly feel that my cock is immersed into something warm, wet and energetic, it could only be Gloria's glorious pussy.

Oh Glory be, it feels so good. Apparently, Gloria fucks with as much fervour as she sucks, because suddenly I feel strangely like I'm in a bull-riding contest, only I'm the bull. I can even picture the lovely, naked Gloria riding my staff clutching her cowboy hat in her outstretched hand.

Her rocking and rolling appear to be contagious for everyone is becoming more passionate. I imagine all four naked cowgirls riding roughshod over various portions of my anatomy. Then I realize I'm in a crucifix position, with beautiful women pinning my head, outstretched arms and groin.

Without warning, Teri reaches orgasm, shrieking and screaming. I hope the crotchety elderly couple next door aren't home. After recovering from numerous waves of short debilitating pleasure, Teri rolls off me and sees that Glory is riding my (her) ramrod with authority.

129

Considering my fuck stick her personal property, she jumps into Glory, knocking her off my (Teri's) passion pole and both of them onto the floor. What she imagined was going on while she was sitting on my face, with her back turned, I have no idea, but she is pissed. In the meantime, Shelly, spying my vacant tallywacker, abandons my left hand and skewers herself upon it. Lisa would like to do the same thing but she is very attached to my wrist.

The fight between Gloria and Teri continues on the floor unabated. I am unable to stop it because a) I am attached, one way or the other to Shelly and Lisa, b) besides, I'm kinda enjoying watching sexy Shelly satiate herself on my Johnny and loose Lisa ride my wrist.

Shelly leans forward, moving in a rocking motion, her tongue caressing my tongue and occasionally laving my ear. Shelly is tighter than Gloria, Teri too, and she is obviously tighter than Lisa, whose snatch, I have not yet entered...with my cock that is. As if to signify that she is still involved, Lisa bends over and starts fondling our hot squirming flesh. While Shelly's pretty pink nipples skirt my chest, matching the same back and forth motion of her pretty pink pussy, Lisa discovers my scrotum and squeezes the testicles tightly. This all is too much for me to take as I begin to experience a slow-growing tingly, tickling sensation that grows and grows into the roar of an overdue extraordinary orgasm. As I spew forth copious amounts of sperm into her hot vagina, I thrash around violently, restrained only by the two women on top of me, whose combined weight may approximate mine.

Apparently my convulsions pushed Shelly over the edge for she was screaming in joy within seconds, matching my lustful thrusts, while grinding her pink taco into my groin as if trying to gain even more of my sizable pleasure pole. Again, I worry about the elderly couple next door. Shuddering from her pleasurable ordeal, Shelly rolls off and snuggles against me. Totally exhausted, I lay relaxing, even forgetting that Lisa is still impaled upon my right fist.

I am suddenly a believer in the maxim – there can be situations where one can have too much of a good thing – as my drained and mildly sore, semi-rigid cock is brutally accosted by a warm, wet sensation and the occasional abrasion of perfect teeth. I gaze down at my groin and once again, Gloria is energetically applying her wares upon my ambivalent love muscle.

'What are you doing?'

'En ettin ooh ard, tso eeh cn uck ig oy.'

'What did you say?'

Glory took a break with her mouth but kept on stroking me and answered, 'I – am – getting – you – hard – so – we – can – fuck – big – boy!'

Lisa was fuming. 'Hey Glor, you had your turn. Now, it's my turn.'

'You'll get your turn. I didn't get to finish my turn cause of Teri. Besides it looks like you're engaged.'

I wonder aloud, 'Where is Ter?'

'This ole street fightin' bitch was gettin' the best of it, so she ran out of the room. I locked the door behind her so she won't bother us no more.'

To my surprise, G-l-o-r-i-a resurrects my resilient erection and of course, climbs aboard, inserting my battering ram into her juicy, tawny twat. As I had previously observed, no one has ever fucked me with more exuberance. Glory was all over the place, constantly changing her motions and style. I want to try other positions, besides Gloria on top, especially doggie style, but I really can't move much with Lisa anchored to my hand. I do have one free hand though, so I titillate the erect half-inch brown nipple of her right tit with my extended forefinger. She bent over and we swapped saliva. I could taste a residue of sex in her mouth, which I assumed was a mixture of Shelly's love juices and my own semen. The idea of the residue of Shelly and my intercourse in Gloria's mouth and now mine further excites me. After about ten glorious, vigorous, hard-fucking minutes Gloria had, wouldn't you know it, a gigantic climax. I would have thought someone had given her a hot foot or hot cunt or a hot something. Much to Lisa's chagrin, I can't help it. I follow Glory with my own megamax.

Pounding on the paper-thin walls forces me to, once again, recall the elderly couple next door. Following the pounding, an irritated, muffled voice 'quiet – ease, –'re – ying to – leep'.

Since Gloria is still vocalizing a combination of shrieking, crying, moaning and groaning. I place my free hand over her mouth, then Lisa lets loose with her own ultimate 'gasm. I take my hand away from Glory's mouth and cover Lisa's, only to hear Glory's enduring screams and more pounding on the wall.

After Lisa calms down, she decides to do something about our predicament. She positions both of her legs against my ribs and shoulder, pushing as hard as she can. After about thirty seconds of strenuous forcing Lisa's super-sized snatch finally releases my hand. It literally popped out with a loud *Thwuunnk*. The corresponding counter-force made Lisa fall backwards off the bed, landing on her back with her well-turned legs extending above the edge of the bed.

Gloria and Shelly think this is hilarious. With both pointing at Lisa's sleek legs, as if to show me what was so funny, they laugh uproariously. I found myself chuckling somewhat also – that is, until the pounding resumes on the wall.

Fortunately, their laughter subsides after that as Lisa regains her footing and climbs back on the bed. She is ready for bear. No make that cock – my cock to be exact. She takes my overworked, shrunken, flaccid cock in her mouth and places her overtly sexy ooh la la at my chin.

I ask you. What's a guy to do? So, I delve into her extraordinary genitalia with newfound vigour. She responds by burying her protruding wishbone shaped clit into my hungry mouth, while giving me a head job supreme. I can tell Lisa's love juices are flowing as an abundance of her tasty fluids enters my mouth, further arousing me.

With nothing to do, Glory and Shelly start massaging my balls and Lisa's tits. Then they begin kissing each other, then rubbing each other's hot spots and soon they are engaged in their own 69 embrace.

I slide Lisa off me. Her unique pussy has been teasing me all night. I will not be denied. Making sure not to disturb Shelly and Gloria, I set Lisa on her hands and knees and enter her from behind. She begins howling loudly and guess what? Once more, there is banging on the common wall. However, I enjoy drilling Lisa's amazing pussy so much, I ignore the banging. After ten minutes or so of hard fucking, the bedroom door opens and there is my beautiful girlfriend.

Teri had put on a robe and an angry face. Her eyes were throwing daggers. I didn't let her glare stop me. I was not about to stop fucking Lisa – she was too hot. I just couldn't understand why Teri was so enraged, after all, I was just engaging in a little All-American fun with her friends. Remember that old saying, 'If you can't fuck your

133

friends, who can you fuck.' If she hadn't been such a stick in the mud, I could have been shtupping her too.

'What's going on here?' an official-sounding female voice says from behind Teri.

Then, as Teri steps aside, two police officers step forth.

'My my,' the woman says, 'isn't this something?'

It's hard to tell in her uniform, but I get the impression that the lady officer is very attractive under all that attire. I read her nametag – H. Orny. *Hmmmm.*

'I think we've come across a bona-fide orgy,' she continued. 'What do you think, Dick?'

By now, Shelly and Gloria have taken notice and sat up, yet I continue to shag Lisa – it is dee-lightful.

My eyes went to Dick's nametag – I. R. Reddy. *Hmmmm.* Dick was a strapping young man in his twenties with reddish brown hair. I noticed two things about Dick. He couldn't take his eyes off Gloria, who happened to be flirting back (the little hussy) and he had a bulge in his pants. *Hmmmm, there are some definite possibilities here.*

Dick answered H. Orny, 'I think you're right Hope. What do you want to do?'

Now my eyes darted back to Hope, hopefully. Hope had taken her cap off and was wiping her forehead with a handkerchief. She was really a remarkable-looking specimen, resembling Jessica Alba.

I spoke up before she could speak, 'Are we breaking any laws here, Officer Orny?'

'No, not exactly. We…we had a complaint from your neighbour, stating there was intermittent…let me see here…moaning, shrieking, groaning, grunting, wailing…' Hope wiped her brow again, then raised an eyebrow, looks coyly at me and continues, 'screaming, wailing, howling and yelling other assorted phrases such as fuck me, don't

134

stop, harder, oh yeah, oh God, oh shit and yes – yes – yes, oh yes, which are keeping the complainants awake.'

As if on cue, Lisa undergoes an enormous orgasmic eruption in which she demonstrates every form of expression that Hope had enumerated, with a few more thrown in. Timing being everything, even though I'm totally worn out, I withdraw my proud, rigid cock, turn to face Hope and stare directly at her while I ask, 'Who's next?'

Hope's eyes become large as saucers. I see her lick her lips then look from my dick to her Dick, who is gaping at Gloria and Shelly. 'Officer Reddy,' I say to get his attention. 'I could sure use some help here.'

Then I grab my staff and glance back to Hope. 'Would you like to be next, Officer Orny?'

Never taking her eyes off my cock, H. Orny says, 'Officer Reddy and I need to discuss this in private.'

Taking Dick's hand they go into the bathroom and shut the door.

Relieved that it wasn't Teri that called the cops, I steal a glance at her. She too is focusing on my grand phallus. She looks up at me and smiles and mouths the words, *I'm sorry,* then shifts over beside the bed, next to where I kneel and starts sucking on me, then deep throating me. While she was doing this, I removed her robe and she was again as naked as the rest of us.

So were Officers Reddy and Orny as they exited the bathroom. Dick, who is well built in more ways then one, if you know what I mean, headed right for Gloria. But it wasn't long before Lisa and Shelly shared Dick's attentions and dick.

Meanwhile, Hope was everything I imagined. Not being a dancer, she was slightly fuller but in an incredible way. Perhaps five six, one-twenty, with brown eyes and long brunette hair, Hope possesses a great tush and sizable upright breasts that bounce ever so lightly as she approaches us.

Beside us, she says, 'I'm next.'

With my dick still in her mouth, Teri's eyes plead with me. 'I'll save some for you too, baby,' I say. Grudgingly, Teri relinquishes my joystick to Hope and leaves the room. I feel sorry for Teri, but I'm not about to stop now.

Hope becomes the fourth beautiful woman I will copulate with in four hours. My girlfriend Teri's pussy is the only one my cock has missed.

For starters, as Teri and each of her friends had, Hope takes Mr Happy in her mouth. I laugh inside as I realize that my joint is being copped by a lady cop. This is obviously not the only prick this beautiful cop has ever copped and after a couple minutes of hardcore fellatio, my cock is back as hard as it gets. Noticing this, she stops, climbs onto the bed, grabs my cock again, bats her eyelashes and with a smile on her lips, demurely says, 'I'm ready for the main course, Mr big cock.' Hope then lays down, staring at me seductively, and spreads her legs wide, pulling me down with her, deftly inserting my cock into her deep, wet cleft.

I must admit this is the first time I ever fucked a cop and I am digging the shit out of it. Not because I was fucking 'the man,' or in this case 'the woman,' as I certainly was, but because she was scrumptious, knew how to use that pussy and wasn't shy. We started with missionary position, then sideways, doggie style, then she got me on my back and shoved her shaved snatch right in my face. I reached up and played with her nipples and she went berserk. I decided women must like head as much as men for each of the five girls had made sure I ate their pussy.

136

Shelly was right beside me, and her sex partner – Dick – was fucking her in the mouth, literally. By that I mean Shelly was just laying there with her head propped up and her mouth open while Officer Dick was doing all the work, shoving his dick in and out of her mouth.

It was about this time when Hope had a seizure like an orgasmic cataclysm. If the other girls were eighty decibels during their orgasms, Hope was ninety db. Like clockwork, the wall began to shake from the sustained banging.

When Hope simmered down, I point to Shelly and Dick and ask her, 'Can we do that?'

'Why not, after that climax, you're entitled.'

We swap places and Hope puffs up a pillow and assumes a recumbent position against the headboard, while, on my knees I stuff her mouth with my guided missile aiming straight for her tonsils. Hope assists by grabbing my scrotum and stroking the base of my cock. I didn't think I could come again but thanks to Hope's expert manoeuvring, I come once more, shooting a load of spunk directly at her tonsils.

After everyone had enough hot sex, Dick and Hope get dressed and say their goodbyes, hugging and kissing everyone. Hope makes sure I have her cell-phone number and Dick does the same with my ladies. We all crash in the king-size bed in a pile of satiated, sexy, hot flesh.

Crazy Has A Name
by Gwen Masters

Until you, I had never done anything crazy.

Until you came along, my tally of insane moments was quite small. I had been drunk exactly three times in my life. I had never had sex outside, or in the shower, and certainly not in a public restroom while people waited impatiently outside. I had never been spanked or gagged with my own panties or treated like anything less than a lady, especially in the bedroom. I was the calm and collected and cool and stable one, the one who was always the designated driver, the one who took care of everyone else. I was the one that was expected to be there but never really noticed.

I was thirty years old and I had lived so quietly, sometimes it was like I had never lived at all.

You, on the other hand, had lived a little too loudly, a little too much. You were the wild child that knew all the best stools in all the best bars, the guy who could get it for you if you really wanted it, the man who had such a reputation with the ladies that you became the silent fear of every man in town.

I remember that day as if it were yesterday. It was an ordinary day and I had gone to do some ordinary shopping. My trunk was filled with paper towels and laundry detergent and groceries. You were walking through the parking lot of the club that I always passed on my way home from the store. You had a long and confident stride, not a swagger but something close to it. You were carrying a paper in one hand and a beer in the other. You held that bottle as though it was a part of you. I watched as you took a long drink, and then you opened the door of that broken-down old truck but, before you did, you looked at me.

The light was green but I hadn't moved. I was mesmerized by you.

You smiled, and interest became lust. I hit the turn signal and steered in your direction.

It was completely out of character for me. You were completely out of character for me. Your hair was too long and your smile was too wicked and your very presence was too overwhelming. You were too young for me, too outrageous for my taste, too irresponsible to fit into my carefully coordinated lifestyle. Yet none of those things seemed to matter when you leaned into my open window that day and offered me a sip of your beer.

There were no words, just the sound of traffic crawling slowly by, others going on to their destinations while we shared a beer in the parking lot in the middle of the day.

It was my first beer. I didn't tell you that, of course. I didn't tell you that I didn't like the taste. I liked the fact that I was drinking what you had just had, that my lips were pressed to the same place yours had been, and ever since then I can't look at a bottle of beer and not think of the way the sun beat down on you that day, turning your brown hair to almost auburn as your smile reached all the way into your green eyes.

Until that meeting in the parking lot, I never dreamed that we would wind up at my place, that you would leave your truck at the bar and get into my passenger seat, that you would be so gentlemanly as to carry the groceries inside, that you would sit and talk with me for hours while I made dinner and cleaned the house and did all the ordinary things that I always did.

You followed me to the laundry room and talked as I folded clothes. You followed me to the backyard as I watered the garden. You chopped onions at my counter, and your hands moved so quickly over the knife that it was obvious – and surprising, somehow – that not only could you cook, but that you enjoyed doing it.

You followed me to the couch, where we sipped wine while the television droned something of little importance and you told me surprising things about your life. You devoured Hemingway and had a soft spot for kittens and worried sometimes that you drank too much. You thought Johnny Cash was the greatest singer who ever lived, and you sang Folsom Prison Blues in your deep and off-key baritone. Then you sang Jackson and I sang along, and soon we were dancing by the light of the television, and when I laughed and told you how much I loved your voice, you stopped singing and kissed me instead.

Later you followed me to the bedroom. I was surprised when you were shy and careful. I had expected that swagger to translate into wanton recklessness, but you were almost hesitant, as though you were worshipping my body and perhaps were not worthy of doing so. You trailed your fingertips over every inch of my legs and my arms and my belly. Everything from my little toe to the top of my ear was kissed. By the time you were done we were both tense as wound springs. The moment you entered me, all caution was thrown to the wind and our lovemaking became an all-out fuck, a hard and vicious

141

coupling that left me with bruises and aches and a smile on my face when the dawn crept through the windows.

You were gone when I awoke. That felt right, somehow. That was just the way it should be.

A week later you appeared on my doorstep with a bottle of wine, and before we were halfway through it you were pouring it over my body and licking up the drops. It left stains on my new carpets. I didn't try to get rid of them.

There was an evening when we ran into each other in the parking lot of the grocery store. We said our hellos and our goodbyes but when I was halfway home there you were, behind me, flashing your lights. I pulled over into the parking lot of an abandoned feed mill and within minutes we were in the bed of your truck, your hand over my mouth and my legs over your shoulders. You fucked me so hard, the truck rocked on its wheels.

Sometimes you stayed with me for days, drinking of that lover's wine. Sometimes you would wake up in the middle of the night and search for me, sighing with relief when you found I was still there, as though I was all in the world that could sustain you. Then one morning you would be gone with no explanations. You probably had other women. I didn't care. All I knew was that when you did come to me, you made me feel more alive than I had ever felt.

And over time, I changed. I learned to drink beer and smoke Marlboros and dye my hair. I learned to curse like a sailor and drive like a maniac and laugh at the irreverence of George Carlin. I even got a tattoo, a little butterfly on the small of my back. Wings outspread in rainbow colors, it looked up at you while you fucked me from behind.

You were my hitchhiker in the middle of the night, my stranger with candy, my loaded gun, my trapeze without a net. You were my crazy.

142

It has been years since that old Thunderbird went off the ravine. The papers said you were drunk, they said you were going too fast, they said you weren't wearing your seat belt. They said all those things in black-and-white headlines, and so they must be true. What they didn't say was that you would always be young, you would always be reckless, and you would always be as perfect for the wrong woman as you always had been, in your legend that would outlive your truth.

Tonight I bought two beers. I drove out to the ravine and drank one of them. Then popped open the other and threw it as hard as I could. The beer splashed out in an amber arc and I waited with bated breath for the satisfying crash of shattering glass.

When it came, I laughed and cried and howled at the moon, just like you taught me to do.

Murder, Whores And Money
by Teresa Joseph

The fluorescent light flickered dimly, leaving the interrogation room so dark that, even if someone had been watching through the two-way mirror, they wouldn't have been able to see a thing. But as Detective Phillips closed her eyes and slipped her tongue into the bisexual hooker's sweet, naked pussy, the woman's groans of ecstasy were more than enough to tell her that she was on the right track.

'Come on now baby.' She purred enticingly, treating the suspect to yet another sensuous *cavity search*. 'Just tell me where you got the money from and I promise that I'll strip search you again.'

The hooker longed to tell her everything. After all, the first time that she'd laid her eyes on Susan Phillips, her pussy hadn't stopped tingling for days. It had been lust at first sight, and she'd been lusting after her ever since.

Lucy might have known that Susan was too damn sexy for her to resist for very long. But although she longed to submit to the gorgeous lesbian detective, the hooker was too scared of her new boss to even dare to breathe a word.

No matter how much Lucy might have tried to resist however, the detective refused to give up. While her interrogation methods might have been against regulations, sooner or later, they always managed to get results.

In the two years since she'd been transferred from homicide to vice, in exchange for turning a blind eye to her offences and a loving, sensuous fuck, Susan Phillips had persuaded Lucy to snitch on her girlfriends, her clients and half of the pimps and hookers who worked in Manhattan South. Because while she might have got a thrill from fucking strange men for a living, she was so bisexual that she could hardly tell the difference. And although it might have been unethical, Detective Phillips was more than willing to exploit it to the hilt.

As a tall voluptuous blonde with a body to die for and a kiss that would have made straight women tingle with desire, Susan was almost eager to use her sexuality on the job.

Every night when she needed information about a new pimp in town, the detective would fix her hair and make-up, put on the sexiest stockings and stilettos that she could find and pay a visit to the alley where Lucy plied her trade. And having found a dark, secluded vantage point where she could view the hooker without fear of being seen, the detective watched her strut up and down under the dull yellow glow of the street light and licked her lips with anticipation as she waited for her to break the law.

Most cops usually complain that stakeouts are long and boring, but Detective Phillips always got such a thrill from spying on the cute young redhead that sometimes it was hard for her to keep her fingers away from her slit.

When push came to shove, the simple truth was that Detective Phillips lusted after the hooker almost as much as Lucy lusted after her. She loved the way the woman dressed. She loved the way she moved. And despite the fact that she was a lesbian, she loved to watch her work.

The moment that the hooker's client handed over the cash, Phillips knew that she had more than enough evidence to swoop down and arrest them both. But biting her lip to keep herself from groaning with delight, the detective would do her best to keep quiet as she observed from the shadows; watching as Lucy squatted down to suck his throbbing cock.

Some hookers might pretend to moan with pleasure to keep their clients happy, but Lucy wasn't faking it. She loved her job. And when the client finally came inside her mouth, she stroked her naked pussy so furiously that the detective couldn't help but join in.

By the time that the man had left the alley, Lucy was always so desperately horny that she was praying for the detective to jump out of the shadows and *arrest* her right there. And sure enough, Detective Phillips was always on hand to make her fondest wish come true.

'Hello again baby.' She'd pant seductively; pushing the lecherous hooker up against the wall and making her '*assume the position*.' And as she slowly ran her hand up the inside of the hooker's thigh and caressed her naked pussy, Lucy always sang like a loose-lipped canary, telling the detective everything that she knew before she even had a chance to ask a single question. But that night when Detective Phillips had visited the alley to pay Lucy another visit, the devoted prostitute was nowhere to be seen.

It didn't take long for the detective to find Lucy hiding out in her apartment. The door had been left open. But for the first time since the day they'd met, when the detective walked into the room, the expression on the hooker's face was one of fear instead of lust.

147

The room was almost completely dark, lit only by a table lamp in the corner of the room where Lucy was cowering, clutching a brown paper parcel as if her life depended on it.

Did Susan need to call for back-up? Was there someone else in the house?

Drawing her weapon from its holster, the detective searched every room in the apartment; she checked the closet, the bathroom, and she even checked under the bed. And having made sure that Lucy was completely alone, she made the woman a fresh pot of coffee and asked her what was wrong.

But Lucy didn't breathe a word. And when Susan sat down next to her and opened up the parcel, she was shocked to realize that it was filled with $50 bills.

'What the Hell is this?' she insisted, hardly able to believe her eyes. Lucy was a two-bit hooker. One look around her dingy apartment proved that there was no way on earth that she could have laid her hands on that kind of money, unless...

The guilt-ridden hooker burst into tears, begging the detective for forgiveness but still refusing to tell her what it was that she had done.

Lucy was beside herself, but Susan could be very comforting when she wanted to be. And after ten minutes wrapped in the detective's loving embrace, Lucy was far too horny to want to cry any more.

'Are you *sure* you don't want to tell me where you got the money,' teased the detective slipping her hand up under the hem of Lucy's miniskirt, forcing her to groan with anticipation and playing the same game that they always played. 'If you don't tell me something soon, then I'm going to have to arrest you again.'

Lucy longed to tell the detective everything. She longed to be rewarded with another loving lesbian fuck. But the moment that she'd taken the money, she'd also known that her new boss would kill her if she talked.

No matter how resistant the hooker might have been however, the detective could also be very persuasive when she wanted to be. And as she made the woman tremble with desire, she knew that it would only be a matter of time before she told the truth.

'Am I going to have to strip search you?' She giggled seductively, slowly pulling down the hooker's spandex boob tube to reveal her gorgeous breasts.

Lucy nodded frantically. But even as the detective wrapped her lips around her pert, swollen nipples, the gasping hooker bit her tongue and refused to say a word.

Even when the detective forced her to '*assume the position*,' slipping her fingers knuckle deep into her naked pussy and forcing her to cum until she wanted to pass out, Lucy still managed to keep her mouth shut. And before too long, Susan realized that she had no choice except to slap the cuffs on her favourite snitch and to drag her downtown.

Lucy didn't mind of course. As far as she was concerned, part of the fun of being a hooker was feeling the cold steel brush against her wrists as she was manhandled into the back seat of a police car. And now that she was being arrested by a lesbian goddess, it was like a dream come true.

Lucy was in heaven, and Susan was enjoying herself almost as much. But after three hours of ceaseless fucking in interrogation room three, Detective Phillips was still no closer to the truth. And so leaving the suspect cuffed to the table for a moment as she paid a visit to the cafeteria, she borrowed a baton from one of the uniformed officers to help move things along.

'Are you gonna' beat the confession out of her?' grinned the uniformed cop as she handed it over.

'Something like that,' she replied.

And thirty seconds later, the suspect was howling with orgasm as the club was rammed into her gushing slit.

'Rachel Whittaker!' panted Lucy, struggling to catch her breath in the brief moment between orgasms as the detective continued to pound her gushing slit. 'She hired me to fuck some guy called Davidson while she photographed us in secret! She sent the pictures to his wife, but then the poor bastard turned up dead!'

'What do you mean?' asked Phillips.

'She's a professional killer, but she pretends to be a PI! She finds rich women who hate their husbands! She tricks bitches like me into setting them up so that she can photograph us together! And then she uses the pictures to get their wives so angry that they hire her to rub them out!'

The detective couldn't believe what she was hearing.

'Why in God's name would you want to go along with this?' she demanded as she threw the baton to one side.

'I didn't know!' howled Lucy, unable to hold back her remorse any longer. 'She said that she was a PI looking for evidence that the wife could use in her divorce! But then when she gave me the money, she told me the truth, and then she told me that she'd kill me if I told anyone else!'

'You have to take me to her,' said the detective as she helped Lucy back up onto her feet. 'Tell her that I hate my girlfriend and that I want her dead; that she's left everything to me in her will but that she's an adulterous bitch.'

But Lucy was adamant.

150

'No Fucking Way!' she insisted frankly, too stricken with terror to care about anything except saving her own skin. 'This isn't some back alley pimp you're asking me to set up! She's a *professional killer*! If she finds out that I'm even here, then I'll be found first thing tomorrow morning with a bullet in my head!'

'Okay, okay, I promise you,' reassured the detective. 'You were never here, we've never met before. But please, tell me everything that you know, and I'll take care of the rest.'

Lucy was still terrified. But having spent the last two years together, she knew that Susan cared far too much to let anything happen to her. And so in spite of her better judgement, the hooker decided to tell the detective everything that she knew.

Even with Lucy's help however, it still took three weeks for Phillips to find the murdering bitch in question and even longer for her to find a way in. But from the moment that Lucy had told her how the two of them had first met, the gorgeous lesbian knew that it was only a matter of time before she could get her foot in the door.

'Hey there honey,' purred Rachel as she pulled up next to the sexy blonde hooker. 'Do you do women as well?'

And even in this dimly lit back alley at ten o'clock at night, the undercover detective was still so shocked by what she saw that could hardly believe her eyes.

The description fit, but if this really was Rachel Whittaker then she looked more like a nursery school teacher than a professional assassin. But then again, that was probably the whole point.

The woman looked so young and innocent that it was hard enough for Susan to believe that she was picking up a hooker, let alone that she might strangle someone with a length of extension cord. But as the thought that she might

151

get away with murder crossed the detective's mind, she put her childish opinions to one side and got on with the job.

'Yeah, I like fucking women,' she giggled, '$10 for a kiss, $20 to lick your pussy and $50 for a passionate fuck.'

And the next thing that she knew, she and Rachel were groaning with ecstasy in the back seat of her car, fucking each other's naked pussies until neither of them could breathe.

'How'd you like to make yourself a few thousand dollars?' asked Rachel seductively, slipping her long, slender fingers deep inside the detective's slit.

'Are you kidding?' gasped the hooker. 'What do I have to…*do*?'

And after several weeks of waiting, the trap was finally set.

As far as Rachel was concerned, Detective Phillips was just another stupid hooker out to make a bit of extra cash. And that, for all the hooker knew, she was just another private investigator out to gather evidence on someone's cheating husband. After all, why would she have any reason to suspect that something else was going on?

Since the day that she'd killed both of her parents in order to claim the inheritance, Rachel Whittaker had learned that playing sweet and innocent was usually more than enough for her to get away with murder.

If she ever got into trouble with the police, or anyone else for that matter, she just smiled and fluttered her eyelashes or cried and pouted until it went away. And since she'd never even been indicted for any of the crimes that she'd committed, to the detective's surprise, her PI's license was completely genuine. But as she continued to play the role that the killer expected her to play, Susan consoled herself with the knowledge that it wouldn't be valid for much longer.

'Okay honey,' smiled Rachel as she and Susan pulled up outside the hotel where she knew that the target would be staying. 'The woman's name is Jennifer Willis and she's arranged for an escort to meet her up in her room for a good hard fuck before bedtime. She's staying in room 314. Here's the key...'

'*Jennifer* Willis?' interrupted Susan 'I thought that we were setting up the husband.'

'Not this time.' She giggled maliciously. 'Her favourite hobby is trawling lesbian night clubs for hot-looking bitches like you. The husband's not too happy about it, and he's going to pay me $50,000 to...gather evidence that he can use against her in the divorce.'

Susan was almost disappointed. Having spent two weeks getting used to the idea of spreading her legs for a man, she'd been curious to find out what it might feel like. But of course, this was no time for her to be wondering about her sexuality. And so, giving Rachel a loving kiss goodbye, she strutted into the hotel lobby and made her way up to the room. But the moment that she got there, she realized that something was horribly wrong.

'Lucy?' she gasped in astonishment. 'What the fuck are you...*Oh my god...RUN*!'

The killer had figured out who Susan really was and that it was Lucy who'd betrayed her. And for the sake of efficiency, she'd decided to kill them both at once.

The mousetrap had indeed been set, but Susan and Lucy were the mice. And although they ran out to the back of the hotel as fast as they possibly could, they knew that the killer could only be a short distance behind.

'Did you bring a gun?' panted Lucy, too busy running to realize just how terrified she really was.

'Sorry darling. I'm undercover.'

But two minutes later when the women found themselves trapped in the hotel's rear corridor, locked in by a fire door that the killer had padlocked shut in advance, Susan wished that she'd taken the risk and put a revolver in her purse.

'What's the matter ladies?' teased Rachel as she slowly strutted up the corridor towards her cowering prey. 'Don't you want to work for me any more?

Susan told Lucy to get behind her. Then taking off her stiletto heels, she prepared to make her move.

'Try it bitch!' snarled the assassin. But before she could even pull the trigger, Susan had thrown the shoes at the ceiling and smashed the fluorescent light.

The corridor was completely black. Rachel fired and Lucy screamed with fear. There were three more gunshots, and then everything went quiet.

'Susan?' whimpered Lucy, cautiously groping around in the dark to find the woman she loved. 'Are you okay?

'Yeah, fine,' panted the detective. 'Are you okay as well?'

Both women breathed a sigh of relief.

'I'm good. What about Rachel?'

'She's dead,' panted Susan.

And in the blinding darkness, the moment that Lucy managed to find the detective's blood-stained hand, the two women embraced each other so passionately that they never wanted to let go.

'Maybe I should get a real job, giggled Lucy, feeling safe and secure for the first time in months now that she was wrapped in her lover's comforting embrace.

'Maybe I should transfer back to homicide,' joked the detective. 'It'd probably be a hell of a lot safer than this.'

Getting Waxed
by Jade Taylor

It would be a lie if I said I'd never fancied girls.

There'd been the girl at school with all the cool clothes, the girl at college with the feathered haircut, Gina Gershon.

But I'd always thought that maybe I didn't *really* fancy them, that it was more an admiration thing, that it was a stage of adolescence as much as bad skin and rampant hormones.

Because after I discovered men those feelings seemed to vanish.

Having a man's strong arms wrapped around you, the feeling of running your fingers across a hairy chest after a bout of energetic sex, the musky smell of cock and a man's sigh as you took him in your mouth; well, what could beat that?

So I was ill-prepared when I saw her, because it definitely wasn't an admiration thing.

I was sitting in the reception area of my beauty salon when I saw her, idly flicking through a glossy magazine.

She had short dark hair that highlighted her delicate features, all high cheekbones and big brown eyes that occasionally glanced in my direction, as if she could sense me looking at her. Every time I looked away, embarrassed to be caught staring, to be caught checking out another girl.

Because that's what I was doing, looking at her lush lips and imagining kissing them, wondering if it was really true that kissing another girl felt that different, that it would feel softer. Looking at her breasts, larger than my own, changing her figure from petite to curvy, wondering what it would feel like to touch them, whether they were as sensitive as my own.

Looking at her cool clothes, her tight jeans and tight black t-shirt so different from my more practical floaty skirt that would allow me to get my bikini line waxed without removing any clothes, wondering if she really were as cool as she looked, wondering if she would be distant if I approached her.

As if I could.

Maybe I was curious, but I wasn't gay, wouldn't know the first thing about approaching another woman. Probably wouldn't even know what to do if she did respond, wouldn't even have the guts to kiss her, let alone anything else.

But it didn't stop me thinking about it.

Maybe it was just because I was off men, I thought, perhaps that was it.

My last relationship had hardly ended happily, and I'd let myself go. Two months of self-imposed exile later and I'd had enough of hiding myself away, and getting out of pyjama bottoms and fat pants, and getting my bikini line waxed and back into thongs was the first step.

Maybe I wasn't ready to get back into the dating game, but at least I could look like I was.

Or maybe I could try something different.

As she discarded the magazine I leant forward to pick it up, ready to ask if there was anything interesting in it, ask her what she'd thought of it, anything to start a conversation.

I didn't know how to chat up a woman, how to do anything with a woman (hadn't even kissed a friend to tease male admirers), but maybe just talking was a start.

'Any good?' I asked, just as my beautician, Kerry, walked towards me.

'Always,' she replied enigmatically, smiling as I blushed.

'I'm ready for you now Jodie, if you'd like to come through?'

I followed Kerry through, making small talk as I quickly climbed on the table, pulling up my skirt to expose my wayward hairs.

The small talk died as Kerry began preparing the wax, I couldn't make idle chat, my head was full of the girl from the waiting room.

Has she seen me looking? Has she sensed my attraction? Was she gay? Or maybe just curious, like me?

I felt nothing as Kerry efficiently slathered on the wax, and just as efficiently placed on the fabric strips to pull it away.

I couldn't help thinking that maybe somewhere else in the building the girl was in the same situation as me, legs spread wide apart, a small thong only covering her modesty, maybe even not that.

I felt myself get wet, and hoped that Kerry couldn't see my thong suddenly moisten as I imagined being there with the girl, touching her while she lay there so exposed.

'All done,' Kerry said, and I quickly pulled down my skirt.

I drove home recklessly, my thong sodden and my clit desperate for some attention. As soon as I got inside I hitched up my skirt and pulled my thong aside so I could slide my fingers inside my swollen wetness. As I touched myself I imagined my fingers were hers, and seconds later I was coming hard, leaning against my door to stop myself falling down.

Six weeks later and I was back at the beauticians.

For six weeks I'd been thinking of her lying in bed at night as my fingers swiftly crept up my thighs to tease myself through my sodden panties, unable to last long before I impatiently slid my hand inside them, inside slick lips to rub my clit hard and fast.

For six weeks I'd been thinking of her as I showered in the morning, soaping up my breasts as my nipples hardened as I imagined her watching, then unable to stop myself as my hands travelled down my body, one hand holding swollen lips apart as the other slid inside me, then back to circle my clit until I came hard.

I suppose in that time my thoughts should have led me to question my sexuality, but they didn't; as far as I was concerned I was attracted to someone and it didn't matter what gender they were.

The only difference was I didn't know where to find her. In my small town if you saw a man you liked they were often far too easy to find, just hang out at the local bars and clubs and before long crossing paths seemed to be inevitable. But she wasn't at any of the bars or clubs (believe me, I looked), and I was too naïve to know where the nearest gay bars were.

So for six weeks I fantasized, hoping, that although it was unlikely, I would see her again at the beauticians; that maybe as her last appointment fell on the same day as

158

mine that maybe this one would too. Maybe as she'd had the same time as me last time, she would again, that maybe that was the only time that was convenient to her, for some unknown reason.

Maybe I was delusional; I like to think of it as optimistic.

So I was gutted when the reception area was empty. Quickly I checked in, picking up a magazine purely so I could hide my face while I ran over fantasies of what might have been.

'Jodie, if you'd like to come through?'

I didn't recognize that voice, I thought as I put my magazine down.

And there she was.

Sure, she looked different in her white outfit, didn't look as cool and unapproachable as last time.

Still looked as sexy.

I licked my lips nervously; what was going on here?

'Sorry, didn't anyone tell you?'

I shook my head wordlessly.

'Kerry's sick. I'm Becca, I'm new here, but I am experienced, so I was hoping you wouldn't mind me doing your wax today?'

I shook my head again.

I followed her through to the back room, she doesn't make small talk and I don't even try.

The room looked the same, but looked so different.

All I could think of was that she'd see me half-naked.

And if that didn't worry me enough, then I thought, she's going to touch me.

I could feel myself getting wet, and knew that, even if Kerry might not have noticed it last time, Becca would.

I was so much wetter, and knew that she'd be able to smell the scent of my arousal as soon she started.

'You know the drill,' she said, gesturing at the bed.

I didn't say a word, just climbed up and pulled up my skirt as she prepared the wax.

'So, any particular style? Brazilian? Hollywood?'

'What's that?' I'd heard of a Brazilian, but not a Hollywood.

'It's when it all comes off.'

I was glad she had her back to me as I blushed madly at the thought.

No way was that going to happen, I wasn't worried about the pain, but there was no way I was losing my thong in front of her, no matter how small it was.

'Just a normal bikini wax,' I stammered, worried I sounded boring, but too afraid to say anything more.

She turned around at last, smiling. 'That's fine.'

I couldn't make eye contact as she touched my thighs, pulled them further apart to position them ready for the wax. As she began the waxing I fixed my eyes firmly on the ceiling, unable to hardly breathe, let alone make small talk.

All I could think about was that she was touching me, my thighs and then higher.

I shut my eyes, worried that she might look my way and see exactly what I was thinking, what I was thinking about her.

That I was thinking about this situation being so different, that I was imagining her bent over me in a totally different scenario, together alone in my room and about to go down on me.

I didn't feel any pain.

I felt myself getting wetter as I imagined her tongue on my skin, getting more turned on every time I felt her bend closer over me.

I didn't know how I'd fuck her, couldn't get my head around the physical possibilities – but still knew I wanted to.

As she pulled off the last strip I knew my thong was soaking wet.

'All done, you okay?' she asked, and I finally opened my eyes, finally dared to make eye contact.

Her eyes were the most brilliant green.

She licked her lips slowly and my mouth went dry.

I licked my lips.

The air between us seemed to crackle with electricity.

All I wanted was to reach out and touch her.

But I couldn't.

'Fine,' I eventually managed to stammer.

Becca smiled broadly.

'Hold on.'

She turned back to her table to grab something.

She returned with aloe vera lotion.

Kerry, my usual beautician, usually put it on after each wax, but she puts it on methodically, quickly, clinically.

This was different.

For a start Becca squirted way too much lotion on her hands. As she put it on I gasped; Kerry warmed it up first, but that was way too cold.

But it still felt good.

Her hands rubbed it in slowly, around the top of my thighs and bikini line, slowly caressed my skin.

My legs were already wide apart, but I couldn't help widening them further.

I could smell my arousal in the air, knew that Becca must be able to smell my musky scent as I felt myself getting wetter, but started to sit up.

161

'That's fine,' I told her, reaching to pull my skirt down, amazingly aroused yet horribly embarrassed at the same time.

She pushed my skirt back. 'Hold on, it's not rubbed in yet.'

Her hands went back to my thighs, went back to massaging in the lotion, getting closer and closer to my thong.

As one hand caught the edge of my thong I moaned in response.

'Sorry, did I hurt you?' She stopped.

I could have said yes, could have stopped it there, but I didn't.

'No.'

'Good.'

She smiled at me again, and continued to touch me.

This time I said nothing as her hand touched my thong, bit my lip to stop myself from crying out.

Then her hand slipped beneath my thong.

Becca started breathing quicker as her fingers slid between my slick lips, finding my swollen clit quickly.

'Becca,' I said, but she ignored me, carried on touching me.

Her fingers slid against my clit, rubbed me softly, and I couldn't help but moan aloud, couldn't help but lift my hips, couldn't help but want her to make me cum.

Then she rubbed my clit harder and faster, and I knew I was going to cum soon.

'Becca,' I moaned again, and then her eyes met mine.

'Yes,' she said, still touching me, watching me as my face flushed, and I could feel my arousal grow.

She licked her lips again, and it was all over.

I came hard, bucking against her hand, moaning loudly.

Afterwards I watched as she turned away to wash her hands, and straightened myself up as if nothing had happened.

I followed her to the reception desk mutely and paid as normal.

She followed me to the door, and I thought, now she'll say something.

Surely she wasn't like that with every client?

Instead she passed me a business card.

'I do home visits too, if that's easier.'

Becca reached over to brush my hair away from my face and although she'd washed her hands, I could still smell myself upon her.

'Okay,' I said, putting the card in my bag.

Two weeks later I phoned her.

'I'd like an appointment please.'

'Wasn't the last wax up to your satisfaction?' she asked, laughter in her voice.

'More than,' I stammered, unable to get my words out now, thinking maybe this was a bad idea, maybe I shouldn't do this.

'So?' she asked again.

'I'd like another appointment.'

This time instead of my usual skirt I was wearing jeans.

As she followed me upstairs to my room I was wet even before she put a caressing hand on my arse.

'So…' I started, certain my nerve would fail.

'So?' she asked, putting her hands on my waist.

'I was thinking of a Hollywood…'

I slipped off my panties.

Night Of The Bear
by Garrett Calcaterra

Silya clutched the brown hair on Varick's chest, using it to gain leverage as she thrashed atop of him. She was skinny, but strong, and one of the few girls he'd been with who could take the whole of him inside her. Part of it, he knew, was the aphrodilium coursing through both their veins; it enhanced sensitivity, somehow turned pain into pleasure. Varick's chest was bleeding where she'd clawed him and torn tufts of hair out, yet the sensation only added to the euphoric energy radiating from his loins.

He bit at one of the pale breasts in front of him, hooking the nipple between his eye-teeth. She gasped and clutched her legs and pussy tighter around him. He groaned and his hips started thrusting upward, in sync with her lunges. She grabbed to his chest tighter and hooked her toes under his thighs, all the while gripping him with her legs and riding him like a bull. All the way up his shaft she'd slide, to the tip of his cock, then slam down onto him again, never letting him pull out of her.

When she came, it was violent: her stomach muscles convulsed, stretching the skin taut. It always set him off. Even as she stiffened and her eyes rolled back into her head, he grasped her waist over her ribs; the muscles

165

inside her contracted around his cock in pulsating waves like she was having a seizure; her knees drove into his kidneys; her fingernails gouged chunks of skin from his chest. He grabbed her ass with his meaty hands and drove up into her with three great thrusts.

Her scream, his deep growl, the slapping of their moist skin together with each collision, echoed off the stone walls of the cellar-like room.

When the white euphoria faded from Varick's eyes and he could think again, Silya was slumped onto him, her head rising with each monstrous breath he took. He was still inside her and could feel warm liquid draining into his fur – partly his own seed, partly her plentiful juices. *Gods, she's good*, he thought, wishing once again he could convince her to leave this place with him. Every time he brought it up, though, she'd just say, *our place is here, my big stupid bear*. He wasn't stupid, and she knew it, but everyone else thought so; that came with the turf being as big as he was and employed as Silya's hired muscle to boot.

A sudden pain shot through Varick's head, and he squeezed his eyes shut. The marks on his chest stung, he realized, and his breath came in short gasps. The phone in the corner started ringing, compounding the pressure building behind his eyes. Varick had a vague recollection of it ringing while they'd been fucking.

'Silya. Silya. The phone's ringing.'

Varick lifted his head and shook her, but she didn't respond. His breath became tighter, and a sickening feeling filled his stomach. He slid out from under her and laid her gently onto her back. He felt her unmoving chest, shook her again, saw the blue hue of her lips. A cramp arced through his side and he cried out, partly in pain, partly from the realization that Silya was dead. The phone

166

was still ringing in the corner. He lunged off the bed mat to snatch the receiver.

'What?'

'Varick? Don't take the aphrodilium. It's tainted.'

It was Dardanio, Silya's associate. 'Too late,' Varick gasped, his chest getting tighter. 'Silya's dead.'

The line was silent for a moment before Dardanio responded. 'Alright, you have a vitropine kit. Get it.'

Varick crawled back toward the bed mat, the receiver still in hand. He swatted away the spent aphrodilium syringe from where it lay on the floor and dug through their pile of clothing until he found the silver metal box. He dropped the phone receiver to open the case and prep the shot. Once the syringe was full, he pointed the needle upward and pushed the plunger until it started to squirt, then picked up the phone again.

'Alright. Just stick it into her heart?'

'It's not going to do her any good, you oaf! Do yourself. We'll take care of her afterward.'

'Right.' Varick dropped the phone. He'd done this a dozen or more times on customers who'd overdosed, but his head was swimming right now, his blood beating in his ears. Spittle was dribbling down from the corners of his mouth into his beard and he knew he was about to lose control. He let himself fall to the bed mat beside Silya and raised the syringe with both hands. He put both thumbs over the plunger and drove the needle down into his chest.

Lightning pain seared through his body. His back arched impossibly and he screamed as his vision went red. Some time later the voice on the telephone brought him back to his senses.

'Varick…Varick?'

Varick yanked out the needle protruding from his chest and grabbed the phone. 'I'm here.'

'Good. Now get dressed. You have to get Silya to a virilis demon.'

'Are you out of your fucking mind?' Varick growled, anger burning away the fog of pain. 'We'll take her to a necromancer to be reanimated. There's one near the harbor. Meet me there with enough money in twenty minutes.'

'Goddamnit, Varick, use that pea-brain of yours! I told you the aphrodilium's tainted. That means someone wants us and our customers dead. You know as well as I do there's only one person…'

Majid. Varick knew better than to say the name over the phone.

'He'll have his men watching all the necromancers,' Dardanio continued. 'They'll be ready to finish off whoever the aphrodilium didn't kill.'

'I'm not afraid of his goons.'

'I am. And I'm the one with the money.'

'You craven piece of shit.'

'I'm a craven piece of shit that will have a long and prosperous life, because I know when to stay hidden away. Now get Silya to a virilis demon so I can get my partner back and figure out what –'

Varick hung up on him. Dardanio was in charge of finances, and the spineless bastard knew Silya didn't keep enough money lying around to pay a necromancer. Varick certainly didn't carry enough cash.

Fuck him! Varick had his own resources. He'd brought in more than a couple of costumers which he dealt with exclusively, a few rich ones he'd sold the new batch of aphrodilium to that morning, in fact. If he could catch one of them before they took a hit and warn them…

He picked up the phone and dialed the first number. No one answered. The second number was the same. The

168

third also. The last call someone answered, but it was some frantic woman, not his customer. He slammed down the phone, shattering the plastic receiver. 'Fuck!'

Kroken the virilis demon was a vile piece of shit. One could usually find him in a corner of the Jade Tavern, swilling whiskey and cheating at cards with whoever was idiot enough to play him. Anyone who called him on his cheating got their heads ripped from their shoulders. The girls that he killed – and sometimes males he really wanted to make suffer – he would drag outside to a back alley to have his way with. None of them ever came back to the Jade Tavern. The barkeep only tolerated Kroken because he paid for the whiskey and because he didn't want his own head ripped off.

The demon eagerly agreed to the small amount of money Varick had to offer him when Varick whispered into his ear who he needed reanimated. Silya and Varick frequented the Jade Tavern often enough, and Kroken always leered at her and made crude propositions she would brush away with her playful quips. As sick as it made him feel to let Kroken have her now, Varick knew he had little choice. It was this or permanent death for Silya.

Under normal circumstances, Varick would never lead anyone to the basement room hidden beneath Silya's pawnshop – the front for her real business. It wasn't the sort of information a dealer wanted to be known, especially by someone like Kroken, but Varick had no intention of letting the demon walk out alive again, let alone spread word of where Silya lived.

Varick had hidden everything away in the room and placed Silya on the bed mat with the covers over her. When he led Kroken down, the demon ripped the blankets away and kneeled to look over her naked body. He ran a long nailed finger up the slit in her mound then stuck it in his mouth before turning to smirk at Varick.

'I'll wait upstairs until you're done,' Varick said, turning to go.

'No. You'll watch. That's part of the deal. I want to you to see her squirm when I stick it in her cunny.'

Varick merely nodded and crossed his arms, not trusting himself to speak. Kroken smirked again then shed his leather vest and trousers. His member was already hard – bulbous and veiny, and mottled black and red like the rest of his skin. Short, black, wiry hair bristled from his well-defined chest and above his cock. He was tall, almost as big as Varick, but with muscles like rocks, not an ounce of fat or softness on him. He grabbed both of Silya's ankles in one hand and lifted her legs up so he could kneel in front of her.

'Are you watching?' he asked as he spat on his hand then rubbed it on his cock. He jammed it in her straight away, not bothering to spread her lips to ease the entry, and her body slid forward on the bed mat, neck craned sideways. 'They don't move around much at first, but the magic button usually gets 'em going.'

Varick clenched his jaw tighter, but said nothing as Kroken snorted down a mouthful of snot and let it drip from his lips onto her mound. The demon started working her clit with one finger, while continuing to thrust in and out of her.

It was imperceptible at first, but colour slowly returned to Silya's face and her limbs stopped flopping lifelessly. After a while, a small moan escaped from her lips and her fingers moved under their own power. Varick stepped forward, but could see she was still not breathing, not alive yet. Kroken continued pounding her, spitting onto his cock

170

whenever it got too dry. When Silya's legs showed signs of life, the demon let go of them to fall to either side of him. Still she didn't breathe and her eyes weren't open, but her hips started rocking and stomach muscles working.

'She's almost there,' Kroken shouted. 'Are you ready for the grand finale?' He pulled his cock out, spit on it again, then lifted one of Silya's legs up and off to the side.

'No,' Varick yelled.

'Yesss,' Kroken hissed, grabbing his cock with one hand and forcing it into Silya's ass. 'YES!' His first lunge was slow, but each successive one faster, more powerful. His hips became a blur. Silya's body arched back. She drew in a deep breath and then she was screaming. Kroken roared. Black fluid spurted from Silya's ass during his last two thrusts, then he pulled out and sprayed more of his black semen, or whatever the fuck he had, all over her.

Varick already had the handgun out and aimed. He waited only to make sure that Silya was living. The moment she took another breath and opened her eyes, he squeezed the trigger.

The shot knocked Kroken off the bed mat, but he was back on his feet almost immediately. 'Fool! You think you can kill me with a fucking gun?'

Varick unloaded the gun on him, every shot in the face. Kroken reeled back into the wall and slumped to the ground. Varick threw aside the gun and was on him in an instant, pinning him against the wall with one foot and looping a garrotte around the demon's manhood. Kroken opened his eyes just in time to see Varick yank on both ends of the cord, severing his balls and member. They flipped up into the air briefly before hitting the floor with a slap. Kroken gasped. Smoke curdled from his mouth and nostrils and Varick barely had time to move away before his body burst into a fit of flames. The demon burned quickly, leaving only a pile of soot, and thankfully setting nothing in the room on fire.

When it was done, Varick turned to Silya who sat trembling on the bed mat. She was covered in the demon's mess and she had shit all over the bedding. Varick was disgusted, but he moved to comfort her anyway. When he got close she smacked him. 'A fucking virilis demon?'

Varick got them a motel room with the money he stole back from Kroken's trousers. Once Silya was cleaned up and Varick explained all that had happened she wasn't so mad at him.

'Majid sold us out,' she told him from where she sat on the bed, wearing only a t-shirt and panties.

'But why kill your best dealers?' It still didn't make sense to Varick.

'Because we refused to deal his new product. *Orgasm.*'

'O,' Varick echoed.

'A crap name. You couldn't have an orgasm if you tried when you're high on that shit. You lose touch with your body, and it's too easy to OD.'

'Ah, that's why I love you,' Varick said. 'You're the only drug dealer I know with scruples.'

'I only sell products I believe in. Aphrodilium makes fucking better and it just so happens that I like fucking.'

'Yeah, well the shit isn't any good when it's poisoned.'

Silya shrugged. 'It was good fucking before I died.'

Varick didn't laugh. She was taking her death too lightly, probably because she was still in shock. The whole thing was starting to make a little sense, though. Silya and Dardanio were Majid's biggest sellers. If they wouldn't carry the O, the other dealers would be hesitant too. Majid would have known that sending out a bad batch of aphrodilium would at the least kill Silya, and maybe

172

Dardanio, not to mention a couple dozen of their aphrodilium users. Word of that would get out on the streets, tainting aphrodilium's reputation, and there'd be even less competition for O. If it was true, Dardanio had probably been right; Majid would have hit men out to finish off Silya and Dardanio and make sure they weren't reanimated.

'Fucking Dardanio.'

'There's nothing more he could have done,' Silya told him. 'We have to find him before Majid does.'

'Majid can have him. We're done with this business. I'm getting you out of town.'

Silya glared at him. 'I pay you, remember? I'm the fucking boss. You do what I say.'

'When it suits me. And right now it suits me to make sure you're safe.'

'You think we'll be safe just because we leave town? Majid has a long reach. There'll be killers after us as long as he lives. If men don't succeed, he'll send wolves or dipsas. As long as he lives.'

Varick took a deep breath. 'You want me to kill him.'

'I want him dead. I didn't mean it had to be you.'

'Who else?'

She didn't answer.

'When I've killed him, we're leaving. We're getting your money from Dardanio and leaving. If Daradanio objects, I'll kill that fucking cock-sucker too and we'll take all the money.'

He went to the door, but she grabbed him before he could leave and pulled his face down to hers. 'Can my furry bear kill Majid?' she asked between kisses. 'He's a moroi.'

Varick pulled away from her, before he got hard. 'Your bear knows how to kill fucking vampires.'

The Pleasure Den was a monstrous neon oasis in the middle of a dilapidated city: part titty-bar, part dance club, part casino, and, if you knew the right things to say to the bouncers, part drug-den and brothel. Majid was the owner and operator. He had his own private suite to entertain lovers and a voracious appetite for teenagers – girls and boys alike – if the rumours were true. Word was that no one could resist his charm when he took a fancy to them. Varick had heard that he took Dardanio as an occasional lover, and that he'd had Silya as well. Silya denied ever fucking him, but Varick wouldn't put it past her. She was young for having risen so high in the ranks.

The place was well guarded. Armed security guards stood at every entrance, the bouncers inside were packing stun guns, cameras were everywhere, and then there were the undercover guards, mulling about in street clothes, drinking and dancing with the other partygoers. Even if sneaky was Varick's strong point, he had no chance of getting inside unnoticed, so he did the next best thing: walked through the front door. The guards paid him no heed and he made his way across the casino floor to the bar he always went to when Silya met with Majid. He ordered his usual, a giant draught of honey ale, and sat there for a moment to make sure the cameras got a good look at him.

When he finished draining his ale, he went to the brothel entrance. Again, the guards wordlessly let him pass, though they patted him down as was their custom. The Madame smiled when she saw him enter the lounge and glided over to take his hand. She was older and wore too much make-up, but had huge breasts that were pressed up and together by her gown and she was not unattractive. Two whores lounged in velvet chairs to his left. One wore a sheer gown of silk that hardly concealed her overly firm fake tits. The other was a redhead and looked more natural, though she wore a more modest nightgown and it was hard to tell for sure. They were attractive, but whores didn't interest him.

'The Bear has finally come to lose himself between the legs of one of my girls,' the Madame said. 'Shall I summon them all for your choosing, or did you already have a particular one in mind? Me, perhaps?'

'Maybe another time. I'm here to speak with Majid.'

She smiled, but the disappointment in her eyes was obvious. She led him past the waiting whores and the ornate staircase leading upstairs to the bedrooms, to the far end of the lounge where two more guards stood before a set of double doors. They frisked him, more thoroughly than the others, and when they were satisfied, let him pass. The room beyond was dim, occupied by twenty or so of Majid's honoured guests, sitting on luxurious floor cushions, or on stools at the bar. Sitar music played quietly in the background. Tapestries adorned the walls. In the centre of the room sat Majid himself. He looked up when Varick entered and for a split second Varick thought he saw a flicker of surprise on his face. *He thought I would be dead, or not so bold if still alive.*

The moroi was cool, though. If he was surprised he quickly recovered and showed no other sign of it. He smiled as he stood and made his way to Varick with inhuman grace. His teeth and eyes shone brightly against the backdrop of his olive skin.

'Welcome, my dear Varick. To what do I owe the honour of your visit?'

'I'd hoped to have a word with you.'

'Of course. Come. Sit with me.'

Varick scanned the room as Majid led him to the expansive cushion in the centre of the room. There were no uniformed guards, but he knew at least four of the guests would be bodyguards, definitely armed, probably in body armour. He'd never be able to kill the moroi before they pumped him full of lead. He'd have to get Majid alone.

'So,' Majid said, 'have you grown tired of Silya's charms?'

'In a sense. She's no longer able to satisfy me.'

Majid merely shrugged, and placed a hand on Varick's leg. 'We all grow tired of our lovers eventually. That's why I have so many. I hope the split won't effect your working arrangement.'

'I don't think it'll be possible for me to work with her again,' Varick told him, but the words seemed to mean nothing to the moroi. All Majid did was frown slightly. 'She's dead to me,' Varick added.

'That bad of a fallout, hmm?' Majid crooned.

The moroi rubbed Varick's leg, and Varick felt overcome with sudden doubt. Either Majid had no idea Silya was dead, or he was playing him a fool.

'Perhaps you can work for me, hmm?' Majid continued. 'I can think of many things the Bear could do in my service. You seem nervous. Tense. Maybe we should talk in private. Hmm?'

Varick was sweating. He'd hoped to get Majid alone, but this was too easy. *Is he falling right into my hands, or am I falling into his?* All Varick trusted himself to do was nod. Majid smiled, then took one of Varick's hands and led him across the floor. Varick wanted to pull his hand free, to not be led through the room like a doe-eyed girl by this man a full foot and a half shorter than him, but he

176

couldn't make his hand let go. His feet were moving unbidden. He looked up and saw the moroi gazing back at him. Once he made eye contact, he couldn't tear his eyes away. It was like staring into the eyes of a god. He was lost in infinitely brown eyes. He could feel himself falling deeper. *He has me*, Varick realized in a panic. *He has no fear of me.* Anger welled up inside of him. The brown eyes were trying to swallow him, and in the periphery he could sense that the music and people were gone, that he was lying down and that Majid was undressing him. Euphoria enveloped him, and for a brief moment he almost gave in – or was it longer? – he couldn't be sure – time lost all relevance – he felt so warm – was this what it felt like to be on O? – was there a reason he was fighting it? – and then he remembered Silya lying on the bed mat dead and Kroken defiling her body, and his rage welled up in him again. He willed his senses to reawaken, his eyes to break free of oblivion.

He regained consciousness with a roar that died in his throat. He was lying naked on a bed and Majid was lying between his legs, sucking his rock hard dick. The moroi looked shocked at first to see Varick staring at him, but then his eyes widened with desire and he went to work on Varick's cock with even more vigour. Varick froze with fear. He dared not move with those vampire cuspids on his manhood. With one hand Majid was stroking the base of his cock, with the other he was cupping his balls and massaging the soft skin behind them, and with his tongue…

Varick collapsed backward and grabbed the headboard with both hands. He was horrified at the thought of being pleasured by a man, of being used by this fucking vampire, yet he couldn't believe how good it felt.

Majid moved both hands to Varick's cock and worked the tip with his mouth. 'No one has ever broke free,' he panted between slurps and tongue curls. 'You will be the first to have me. You, the Bear, will take me.'

Sudden understanding washed over Varick. *He's seduced hundreds, he's fucked them, but never been fucked.* He wasted not an instant. He grabbed Majid's thick mane of hair in one hand and shoved down, burying his cock in the moroi's throat. When he felt him gag, he yanked his head up into the air and stared him in the eye. Varick still held tightly to the headboard with his other hand.

'I'm gonna fuck you now.'

Majid nodded eagerly. 'Yesss.'

Without warning, Varick yanked Majid to the side of the bed by the hair, and with his other hand snapped off a section of the bedpost and slammed it into the moroi's heart. Majid gasped and shook his head slowly as he looked up at Varick.

'Why?'

'Because you tried to kill Silya.'

'No, no, no,' the moroi said. 'Not…Kill…Silya…'

Varick sat back and watched as Majid died, repeating 'no' over and over again. Varick had never known a man to lie while in the throes of death, and he was overcome with an unsettling feeling. It wasn't remorse; if for nothing else, the bastard deserved death for trying to rape him. No, it was that none of this added up. Majid never once let on he knew Silya was dead, and he wasn't that good an actor. Varick had caught him off guard twice. No, he knew nothing about the tainted aphrodilium or Silya dying. *Who else then?* The answer was obvious enough. *Dardanio.* He was the one who called and told Varick to take Silya to a virilis demon. He would have known she'd send Varick after Majid. *But who does he want dead? Me or Majid?* It could have been one or both, and now that Varick thought about it, he realized he was far from out of harm's way. He was still in Majid's lair, and once someone realized what had happened, every god-damned guard in the place would be after him.

He hopped from the bed, grabbed his clothes, and surveyed the room. There was only one door, the one leading back into the private bar lounge, but also a security monitor screen at a desk. He went to the monitor and toggled through the security camera feeds while putting on his trousers. There were a half dozen feeds from the casino, one at each of the eight bars, two in one of the men's restrooms, one in the brothel lounge, two in the private bar lounge, three in the drug den, one in a control room…Varick stopped and looked closer at the screen. There were guards in the control room and someone else. *Dardanio.* They were looking at their own monitors. Varick toggled the switch again and saw himself on the screen. He looked up at the ceiling, and sure enough, there was a camera in the corner, a little black half-circle eye in the sky.

Varick moved for the door, but it opened before he got there. It wasn't a guard that stepped into the doorway, though. It wasn't Dardanio. It was Silya. She leveled a gun at him. His gun. The door closed behind her as she stepped inside the room. She was wearing her work clothes. Black leather pants and tight tank top. No bra. She'd learned a long time ago she had the upper hand when a customer or enemy was preoccupied staring at her tits.

'Silya. What are you doing here?'

For an answer she shot him. He fell back onto the floor, more out of shock than pain. The bullet had missed his heart, only pierced one of his lungs, and he was able stay up on one elbow.

'I knew you could do it, my big stupid bear,' she said, walking closer. 'Dardanio didn't believe me, but I told him you would.'

Varick felt sick. 'Majid never tried to kill you.'

'Of course not. He was too vain to realize he should have killed me. But we taught him a little lesson about that, didn't we? Did he take you in the ass before you killed him?' She glanced at Majid's corpse, and saw that it was still clothed. 'Impressive.' She yanked Varick's arm out from beneath him and he crumpled to the floor.

'Why?' he groaned.

'Because, you stupid bear. Majid has no second in command, no heirs. Dardanio is next in the line of succession to inherit his empire.'

'Fuck Dardanio.'

'Dardanio's my partner. He's practically raised me in this business.'

'Fuck Dardanio,' Varick grunted again. 'He's a fucking pussy. I love you.'

Silya smiled. 'And I love the way you fuck me. For that, I'll make this moment sweet for the both of us.' She threw aside the gun and pulled a zipper pouch from the back pocket in her pants. She opened it and prepped the syringe, then shot him up with aphrodilium. 'The last of the tainted batch,' she said as she unlaced her pants and slid them down her slender white legs. She wore no panties, and her clean-shaved mound was still pink from her earlier encounters that day.

Varick was already hard when she yanked his trousers away. She teased him, though. Licked at him first, barely brushing the tip of his cock with her tongue. Then she danced slowly over him, lowering her swaying hips, almost touching her pussy to his cock, then his face, letting him smell her. She pulled her shirt up, exposing her flat, muscled stomach, but she wouldn't bare her tits for him. She knew how he loved them.

She hovered back towards his cock and lowered herself onto his legs, then slid her mound across his cock so that it pressed up against his stomach. She got wet then, and could hold out no longer. She slid down onto him, began rocking her hips. He couldn't help but breathe in deeply. He hiccupped blood, but the aphrodilium had washed away the pain of his gunshot wound. He let his head fall back and closed his eyes, trying to remind himself she had betrayed him. Used him. Was trying to fucking kill him.

'Wasn't I good to you?'

'Too good,' she panted. 'Too stupid. I don't need a fucking knight in shining armour to steal me away.'

She licked her finger and jammed it into the bloody hole in his chest. It hurt like hell, even through the aphrodilium, and with that, whatever feelings he had for her were swept away. He grabbed her arms and rolled over with a grunt, so that he was on top. Still, she never let him come out of her. Now he was doing the thrusting, though. Her legs flopped up in the air as he drove into her. He could feel the pressure building in his balls and at the base of cock. The fucking vampire blowjob had been a horrible tease, and he felt ready to explode. He ripped her shirt away and sucked at one of her tits. She wrapped her legs around him and pulled him into her harder.

'That's right, my big stupid bear. Fuck me hard when you die.'

Varick could feel the blood rage overtaking him. 'You stupid bitch. I am a bear.'

'Yes, my big stupid bear. Fuck me harder.'

The hair on his arms and chest was standing on end, and he knew he was losing control. 'I'm a fucking berserkr,' he tried warning her. 'Your poison won't kill me.' It was too late, though. She was gasping and her cunt muscles clenching around his cock. He let himself go as he exploded inside her. He heard himself roar and that was the last thing he remembered.

When he regained consciousness he was covered in blood. He was no longer in Majid's room, but rather in the casino. The mangled corpses of two dozen guards were strewn about him and Dardanio's messily severed head was lying at his feet. All the guests had fled and Varick was the only living person in the Pleasure Den as far as he could see. He thought of going back to Majid's room, but decided he didn't want to see what he'd done.

It'd been almost five years since he'd last let himself shape shift. He didn't like losing control, but Silya had left him no choice. He'd tried to take her away, but she wanted nothing of it, and never really wanted him, he knew now.

Varick looked his naked body over. He had a couple of gunshot wounds, but they'd heal, just as the one Silya had given him already had. He didn't even feel the after-effects of the tainted aphrodilium.

A sudden commotion to his left caught his attention, and he turned to see the Madame and a couple of half naked whores burst from the door leading to the brothel. They screamed and ran when they saw him. He could do nothing but laugh. Even whores were afraid of a berserkr.

What's the matter? You said you wanted the fucking bear.

Personal Enquiries
by J. Carron

'It's like that ship…what's it called again?'

Danny has never been much good at general knowledge. That's why he never makes it into the station's pub quiz team – he's reserve number four.

'The Marie Celeste,' Claire points out.

He's right though, she thinks to herself. The back door was wide open when they arrived at the scene. There are two coffee cups on the kitchen table and a newspaper spread open. There's even a packet of biscuits and a pint of milk out. She notices the milk's off; it smells.

'Either they're very trusting, or they had to leave in a hurry,' he says, loosening his tie.

Danny looks uncomfortable in that cheap polyester suit. Perhaps it's the fact his neck's too fat for his shirt collar, or his belly's too big for his belt. She wishes he'd lose weight and smarten himself up a bit.

Claire wanders through to the hallway. She picks up the pile of letters sitting behind the front door, sifts through the envelopes. There's an answering machine on the table, a red light flashing up the messages waiting to be heard.

Danny joins her. He's flicking through his notepad.

'What have we got then?' she asks impatiently.

'The postman contacted us. He was delivering a parcel. There was no answer when he knocked so he went round the back to leave it on the back doorstep. The door was wide open and when he shouted out, no one answered.'

'Do we know anything about the people who live here?'

'I talked to the neighbours. They say they're a quiet couple, Paul and Elaine Harrison. They keep themselves to themselves. They've got two kids but they're away at boarding schools for most of the year.'

'The amount of letters suggests the Harrisons have not been here for a few days,' she ponders. 'See if you can find out where they work. They must have good jobs if they can afford this place and send their children to private school.'

Danny lumbers off obediently. Claire checks out the various rooms of the house, finishing her cursory search in the lounge. It's a large room, well furnished with a cream leather suite and a giant plasma screen TV. She's envious. She'd love to live in a house like this, but her force salary will only stretch to it if she climbs the ranks. Detective Sergeant is fine for now but she needs to escape this staid rural backwater if she wants to get ahead.

Beneath the TV there's a DVD player. She notices the tray is open, a disc sits in it. There are words written on the disc in black permanent marker. She kneels down and reads them. *Home Movie, No 1*.

She's intrigued to see what they look like, the Harrison family. She decides it will help her in her enquiry if she can put faces to the names. Claire flicks the TV on and nudges the tray into the DVD player. She expects to see the family celebrating Christmas or a birthday, or enjoying a special day out. Instead she sees a couple sitting in the front of a car, a large 4x4 by the looks of it. It's light outside and there are trees in the background. The camera looks as if it's positioned on the dashboard.

She hears his voice first. 'I want you, babe!'

The woman's left hand roams onto his chest, fingers slipping between the buttons of his shirt, massaging the bare skin beneath with slow, deliberate strokes. All the while she holds his gaze with wide eyes.

His hands encircle her narrow waist, pulling her onto him so she sits knees apart across his thighs, her back pressed against the steering wheel, her groin thrust against his.

'I love you, Paul,' she whispers in a husky tone, gyrating lightly against him.

'Elaine,' he sighs almost breathlessly, his hands wandering tentatively under her chunky-knit sweater, seeking out the taut, milky-white flesh below.

'I want you. I want to fuck you.'

She hauls her jersey off and tosses it onto the passenger seat. Tousled strands of black hair cascade down over her face like the dark grain of white marble. He sinks his face into the shallow valley between her breasts, nuzzling the gently rounded curves. Her body quivers. She moans softly, throwing her head back as he unclips her bra and runs his dewy tongue over her nipples.

Her hands are on the waistband of his trousers, unhooking his belt, zipping the fly down and pulling the material sharply back. He fumbles with the fastener on her jeans. It looks so cramped in the car. She brushes his hands away, rises up and unhitches them herself. He helps her pull one leg free of the denim as she takes his hard cock in her palm, easing him up towards her pussy as she sits astride his hips once more and plunges down onto him with a hissed intake of breath.

Claire watches as they make love on the front seat of the car, Elaine Harrison rising and falling with long, painfully slow arcs of her body, the stretched curves of her chest pushed out to meet Paul's mouth as his hands drift over her stomach and hips, occasionally dipping lower to add to her mounting pleasure.

The fucking gets faster and more frantic. Elaine shrieks as she rides his prick harder.

'What you got there?' Claire hears Danny's monotone voice, suddenly realizes she was too wrapped up in watching the sex to see him enter the room.

'Er…just a DVD,' she stutters, hitting the stop button on the machine.

She pops the disc out and slips it into an evidence bag.

Claire sits at her desk reviewing her newly opened file on the missing couple. Normally it would be treated as low priority, but there isn't much else happening in CID so she decides to run with it until a more juicy case comes along. Danny is sitting opposite, munching on a hamburger. She winces as she watches him stuff his face.

His phone rings. He wipes the back of his hand over his greasy chops and answers. A moment later he hands it across the desk to Claire.

'It's for you, someone wanting to speak to the officer in charge of the Harrison case,' he explains.

Eagerly she picks up the handset.

'DS Claire Reid, how can I help?' She hears nothing, other than the sound of the line going dead. She hands it back to Danny.

'Strong silent type?' he suggests.

She tries to trace the number, hopes the caller might have vital information on the whereabouts of the Harrisons, but to no avail.

*****

Back home, Claire rustles up a bite to eat – another microwave meal for one. She uncorks a bottle of red wine and savours the fruity taste. She eats hurriedly and, immediately after supper, powers up her laptop. She inserts the DVD. The Harrisons have been on her mind all day. How could a couple just disappear and not be missed by anyone? Paul Harrison did tell staff at the factory he owned he was taking a couple of days off, but that was almost a week ago and there was no mention of any imminent holiday plans.

Then there was the DVD, left sitting in the machine. Who left it there? Surely the Harrisons would hide something so personal. If it was hers she would. It's playing now, the footage she viewed before she was so rudely interrupted by Danny.

Claire watches intently, following the couple's every move. Elaine, she estimates, is in her mid-thirties, slim and attractive, with a taut, supple figure. Paul is a little older but Claire can see he clearly takes care of himself. He's fit and muscular with a healthy tan.

They look like the perfect couple.

The sex reaches a climax. Elaine shudders uncontrollably as Paul makes a final long, stabbing upward thrust. She grabs his hair, hauls his face into her cleavage and cries out. Claire sees Paul's hips stiffen beneath her. They remain together for a long, lingering moment, their bodies glistening with perspiration.

They pant breathlessly until at last she prises herself from him, floats back onto the passenger seat.

Claire watches as she repositions the camera slightly, zooms the lens in on Paul's still-hard prick. It's the first time Claire has seen the erection clearly. She's transfixed; she can't take her eyes off the screen. She's never viewed pornography before, never felt the need. She's always seen it as something only men look at. But this shot arouses her. It's so clear she can see the glossy sheen of blended love juice coating the shaft.

Elaine lowers her head into her man's groin and gently guides his cock between her lips. She rolls her tongue around the head, its tip probing the narrow slit, flicking relentlessly back and forth over the polished red flesh.

Claire cannot see Paul's face but she can tell by the noisy grunting and groaning that Elaine is skilful in her handling of his manhood.

Claire's hand is on her crotch, its journey there bred of desire. She feels very hot, flustered. There's a moist warmth between her legs, a tingling aching to be nurtured.

She slips her palm under the waistband of her jeans, onto her knickers. The warmth radiates against her fingers, inviting them in.

Her gaze remains on the screen, studying Elaine as she takes Paul into her mouth, her silky lips gliding effortlessly down the rigid muscle, enveloping it whole.

Claire's forefinger brushes against her clitoris. She feels its tiny head poke up between the folds of her labia. She caresses it gingerly through the fabric. She's done this many times before, in the privacy of her bedroom.

But this is the first time she's watched strangers fucking and touched herself. She increases the pressure, rubs more vigorously as her eyes follow Elaine's lips up and down.

His moans of undiluted pleasure fill her head as she rubs harder and faster, her own lonely world dissolving into the action before her.

Claire closes her eyes, pictures her own mouth wrapped around his cock. She responds willingly to his desire, concentrating her lips and her tongue on the source of his joy, speeding up her rhythm when his sighs threatens to subside, slowing down when he grunts harder and she senses he's about to come. She teases out his pleasure painfully, makes him wait for that inevitable moment.

She knows she can make him come; she knows she has the power to decide when.

She can hear his moans grow in pitch again.

She feels his cock twitch and his balls rise.

Will she prolong the excruciating agony of an orgasm denied or release him, let him enjoy the fruits of his labour? She decides to let him go, savours the taste of his warm sperm as it explodes into her mouth, ebbs and flows inside her, coating her tongue and dribbling down her throat. Elaine is watching, smiling, as Claire comes, too. Her orgasm is one of the most intense she can remember. But as she opens her eyes the ecstasy dies instantly, its place taken by a deep sense of guilt. What the hell is she doing masturbating over a film of two people who, for all she knows, could have been abducted or worse still, be dead?

'Where did this come from?' Claire asks, lifting the package from her desk. It has her name written on it, but no postage stamps.

'It was handed in last night,' Danny replies.

'Who by?'

He shrugs his heavy shoulders unhelpfully.

Claire tears open the envelope and a DVD drops out. It's marked, *Home Movie, No 2*. Immediately she recalls the guilt of the previous evening, the shame of climaxing over a film – bagged as police evidence – of two missing people having sex.

'Get me a coffee,' she barks.

Once Danny is out of the room she slots the disc into her computer. Elaine has the camera trained on her husband as he climbs out of a dark blue Range Rover.

Claire can hear her voice in the background, urging him on. They're in a car park, not in town but in the countryside. She thinks she recognizes it and her suspicions are confirmed when Paul walks over sand dunes to a beach. It's a beauty spot about twenty miles down the coast.

Paul and Elaine are alone on the beach.

From what Claire knows of the area it doesn't surprise her. It only attracts bathers in the peak of summertime; for most of the year only surfers, ramblers and dog walkers go there.

The couple stop at an upturned boat.

Elaine places the camera down on the hull and appears in the frame alongside her husband. She wears a camouflage green top and a white miniskirt. She flirts with the camera, dances provocatively in front of the lens.

Paul smiles encouragement as her lithe hips gyrate. She rotates them slowly, thrusts her groin back and forth lustily. She slides her skirt up over her thighs, teases the camera with her posturing. There are no panties beneath, just a neatly trimmed mound.

Who is sending her this stuff? What kind of twisted mind, she wonders, is getting off on posting her films of a missing couple at their most intimate? Is it some kind of bizarre message, the forerunner to a ransom demand?

She continues to watch. Paul's jeans are round his ankles. He lines himself up behind his wife, takes her waist in his hands and tugs her skirt right up so Claire can

190

see his bobbing cock slide into her silky cunt. They go at it hard, breathless fucking on the beach, both staring into the camera.

The Range Rover is in the beach car park when Claire arrives. She screeches to a halt next to it and leaps from her car. The big 4x4 is empty but she notices her tormenter has left a silver disc below one of the wiper blades.

He's creating a trail for her to follow. She grabs it and dives back into her car. She brought her laptop, knowing she might need it.

The film begins with a shot of an old beach hut, paint peeling from the wooden facade.

Suddenly Elaine darts past the cameraman into view. She's barefoot, but still wearing her camouflage top and white skirt. She stops running, turns briefly to face the camera, flashes an inviting smile, her forefinger beckoning the viewer on, then she's off again, skipping across the sand towards the tiny hut. The camera follows but stops when she turns again.

'Come on.' She winks before scampering off again.

The Harrisons enjoying happier times.

Claire runs down onto the beach. She stops, looks left, then right. There's no one about, but she spots the wooden hut. She's off again, sprinting along the sand towards it.

Her mind is racing, too, trying to determine in advance what she might find. Is the captor holding his victims there? Will she find another disc, another clue? Is this just another step in an increasingly bizarre game of cat and mouse?

Claire slows as she reaches the hut. She wonders whether she should call for back-up.

But there's no sign of anyone around, no one keeping watch. She creeps up to the veranda on the front of the shack, her heart beating faster, her breath shallow. She steps onto the rotting wood, eases her body towards a window. Her back is to the wall now, the window to the left of her shoulder. She edges closer, swivels her head to look through the glass.

She sees two people inside, recognizes them immediately – the Harrisons. And they're fucking on a rug spread across the floor. Claire's anxiety suddenly turns to anger.

She bursts through the door. Paul looks round, sees her, but continues to hump his wife, his arse bouncing up and down between her spread thighs. He simply greets Claire with a smile, holds her astonished stare.

'We wondered if you'd come and join us,' Elaine moans between long-drawn-out sighs.

'Pity she's not in uniform,' Paul groans.

'What the hell is going on?' Claire demands. But they're too wrapped up in shagging the living daylights out of each other to answer. He looks to be on the verge of shooting his load and by the sound of it Elaine is about to come, too.

'I'm a police officer,' Claire shouts. 'Stop it!' Her protestation just spurs them on.

Together they reach orgasm. Claire doesn't know what to do. Her training never prepared her for anything like this. She's out of her depth.

'Wow, that was amazing,' Elaine sighs as Paul finally rolls off her.

'Best yet,' he agrees, panting like a dog.

'What do you think you're doing?' Claire roars.

'Something impulsive,' Elaine beams.

'Something so spur of the moment, so risky it's dangerous.'

'Did you send the discs?' Claire asks.

192

They nod in unison. She notices how Paul's cock twitches every time she speaks.

Suddenly the penny drops – she realizes she's been drawn into their sex games, her presence fuelling their voyeuristic fantasies. It all makes sense: the discs were an invitation to her to watch, to become involved. And she has on both counts. She's watched the films, not just once but repeatedly, and she's touched herself, brought herself off as she did.

'It was just a bit of fun,' Paul says, apologetically. 'Let us make it up to you.'

'I ought to arrest you for wasting police time,' Claire warns, taking out her handcuffs…

Danny's at his desk when Claire arrives for work the following morning. She's late, by ten minutes. It's the first time she's ever been late in her life. She plonks a takeaway coffee in front of him. He's surprised by her sudden generosity.

'Heard you found them,' he grunts.

'It was all just a misunderstanding. They'd gone away for a few days together, that's all.'

'So no arrests?'

'No.' she smiles. 'I dealt with them myself.'

Test Drive
by Roxanne Sinclair

As Nigel watched Cathy skip down the driveway he wondered if he should have a word with her father about the appropriate dress code for a person having a driving lesson. But maybe when you were seventeen a skirt the size of a belt and a blouse open three buttons at the top might be an appropriate dress code. Plus how do you tell your best mate that his daughter's erect nipple nearly had your eye out last week?

Nigel got out of the car and walked around the back so that he could climb in the passenger side.

Cathy walked around the front dropping one hand onto the bonnet, allowing her fingers to caress it as she moved. Her other hand was on the crisp white collar of the blouse that she was almost wearing.

'Hiya, Nige,' she purred.

'Cathy.'

There was a moment, when they locked eyes. His were brown pools of misery for something he wanted but knew he could not have. Hers were a sapphire challenge of come on if you dare.

Feeling the rising flush in his face, Nigel was the first to break the look as he pulled his eyes away. He had time to close his door and fasten his seatbelt before Cathy finally poured herself into the seat beside him.

'Are you nervous about your test?' Nigel asked.

'Should I be?' Cathy twirled a loose curl around her finger and looked at him from beneath her long eyelashes. 'You're a good teacher.'

He forced himself to concentrate. 'Make yourself comfortable Cathy, then, in your own time, pull out into the traffic please and drive straight ahead.'

Cathy, blonde and built to thrill, adjusted her seatbelt so that it lay in between her breasts.

Nigel glanced sideways in the pretence of looking behind but in reality his eyes made it no further than those tight breasts. Their freedom beneath her blouse was obvious and her nipples looked like tiny erect buttons.

She pulled at the hem of her skirt in a vain effort to pull it down over her smooth thighs.

Nigel watched her efforts out of the corner of his eye and then allowed his gaze to wander down her thigh to the bend of her knee and then to her muscular calf as she depressed the clutch and put the car into first gear.

He did his best to keep his eyes on the road ahead but found his gaze constantly straying.

By the time the car had rounded the end of the street he could already feel beads the size of house bricks forming on his forehead.

'You hot?' Cathy asked.

'A bit,' he admitted as he wound the window down.

He could feel Cathy's eyes on him.

'I'm feeling a little warm myself,' she said, the tip of her tongue sliding between her lips.

Nigel cleared his throat. 'Eyes on the road, Cathy,' he said adopting a professional tone. 'That'd be an instant fail on your test.'

He saw what he was looking for. 'Pull up along the parked cars on the left please, Cathy and reverse into the parking space.'

Once at a standstill beside the parked cars, Cathy shifted in her seat so that she was sitting sideways to the steering wheel.

'Is this position all right?'

'Yes,' he answered quickly.

'You haven't even looked,' Cathy pointed out. 'I need to get the position right otherwise I won't be able to do it properly.'

Nigel looked over cautiously.

Her hands on the steering wheel meant that her arms pushed her breasts together and formed a deep cleavage.

He quickly dropped his eyes and they landed on her skirt. The positioning of her feet on the pedals meant that it had ridden even higher on her thighs and afforded him a glimpse of her white panties.

'Well?' she asked.

'Your position's fine,' he said with a voice that barely rose from his dry throat.

All the while she was manoeuvring the car slowly into the gap his gaze strayed to her cleavage.

'You're not looking where I'm going,' Cathy laughed.

'I thought you wanted me to check out your position,' Nigel said without taking his eyes off her tits.

He questioned whether he was misreading the signs: no. He was sure he was not. Every lesson was the same.

With the car parked Cathy asked. 'Do you remember that place we used to go to when I first started having lessons?'

'I'm not sure.'

'That place where there was no one around.'

Her smile was like a bolt of lightning through his body. He wondered how much longer he'd be able to resist what was on offer, and had been since her first lesson.

'The old aerodrome?'

'Yeah, will you take me there?'

'Why?'

She looked at him under lowered eyelids. 'There are some other manoeuvres I'd like to try out.'

Nigel worried for a split second about the manoeuvres of his own he'd like to try out up there. He knew they were the same as hers but…his best mate's daughter?

Fuck it, he thought dismissing his doubts. No, he changed his mind. Fuck her.

'If you're sure,' Nigel said with the knowing smile of a middle-aged man who knew he was about to shag a seventeen-year-old.

The disused aerodrome was by its very nature a quiet place. But just in case there should be anyone about, he directed her to the farthest point from the main gates. There were a couple of square acres of trees around the perimeter.

Following his instructions, Cathy pulled the car to a halt and turned off the engine.

The bravado she'd shown all the way there and from day one disappeared. She looked straight ahead out of the windscreen.

Nigel, remembering who he was, who she was and what was on both of their minds asked. 'Do you want me to take you home?'

'Why?' Cathy seemed hurt.

He looked at her breasts as he spoke. 'Because you're seventeen, you're my best mate's daughter and you might have started something you don't really want to finish.'

'I haven't,' she whispered, lowering her eyes.

'You sure?'

'What's the matter?' Cathy asked defensively. 'Don't you fancy me?'

Nigel's answer was to lean forward, cup her face between his hands and kiss her.

When she didn't respond he pulled a few inches away and looked at her.

She looked at him and then she was the one to do the kissing and he responded, gently at first, but then with increasing urgency.

He moved his lips from her mouth to her throat. As his right hand held the back of her head his left hand played with the buttons of her blouse. He was not as expert as he would have been with his right hand but he managed and soon the edges of her blouse fell apart and her breasts were completely exposed.

Their shape was perfect, if a little larger than what he was used to, with erect caramel coloured nipples sitting just high of centre on each of them.

Moving his hand to cup her right breast, he followed its curve with his finger all the way round until the nipple, now more proud than ever, barred his path. After flicking at it gently, he lowered his head.

With the sweetness of Cathy's perfume filling his nostrils he gently nibbled while his hand followed the curve of Cathy's body until he felt the outline of her panties. He broke the gentle resistance of the elastic with his finger and moved along until his finger rested on her soft mound.

Cathy stroked his hair like he was a faithful dog.

Feeling the rising within himself, Nigel pushed himself into an upright position.

'What's wrong?' she asked.

'Cathy,' he said seriously. 'If you come with me into those trees, I am going to throw you on the ground and fuck your brains out.' He smiled at her. 'Will you come?'

'Thought you'd never ask,' she said with her old confidence fully restored.

'But there's one thing you're going to have to remember,' he said as he opened the door.

'What's that?'

'I'm the teacher and you have to do exactly what I say.'

She smiled. 'Okay.'

'And the first thing is that you leave that blouse as it is.'

He walked around the back of the car and opened the boot. As he lowered it after taking out the blanket that he kept there he saw that Cathy had followed his orders. She stood by the side of the car with her blouse lying either side of her exposed breasts.

He motioned her to follow as he led the way into the trees. There was a patch of ground covered in moss and that was where he lay the blanket down.

They stood looking at each other. Both of them wanted what was coming next but only one of them was in the driving seat. Teacher and pupil.

'Take your blouse off,' Nigel said as he unbuttoned his shirt. Both garments fell onto the floor.

'Now the skirt,' he instructed as he pulled his belt free from his trousers at the same time as he kicked off his shoes.

They stood wearing just their underwear. Hers a tiny white thong and his stripy boxers that failed to contain his huge erection.

Cathy looked at the stalk that he had grown with wide eyes.

It pleased him.

'Come here.'

She obeyed immediately. The tips of her breasts brushed his chest.

'Take them off,' he said.

Cathy took hold of the side of her panties.

'No,' Nigel said.

She looked startled. 'Mine.'

'Oh,' Cathy's coyness could have been mistaken as genuine.

She fell onto her knees, her face inches from his groin. Grasping the band at the top of the boxers she pulled.

As they came down Nigel's penis was forced downwards: once released it bounced against her face before returning to its almost vertical position.

'Rub it,' he commanded and she took it in her small hand and rubbed along its full length. After she had rubbed it for a few minutes Nigel instructed her to 'put it in your mouth and suck.'

Cathy had just been waiting for the instruction because she obeyed without hesitation.

It occurred to him that this was not the first time that Cathy had taken a cock in her mouth. Either that or she was a natural.

She used her cheeks to suck, her teeth to scratch and her tongue to do God knows what.

Nigel threw back his head, unable to hold himself in check. It had been a long time since anyone had done this. He shot his load quickly.

Cathy swallowed his juice hungrily like someone who hadn't eaten for a week.

As she wiped the remnants of his spunk from her lips she looked up at him and smiled. 'Tasty.'

'Stand up.'

With her lips slightly open just inches from hisr face Nigel opened his mouth and kissed her. His tongue searched for hers and he could taste his own saltiness in her mouth.

His hands went to her breasts and he took a nipple in each hand. He tweaked them gently, before releasing them and moving his hands down to her crotch.

As he gently rubbed he felt his temporarily flaccid member come back to life.

He pulled his lips away from hers. 'Your turn,' he whispered and he fell to his knees.

At first he just looked, then using just his thumbs he traced the outline of the V at the top of her legs, and then slowly he tugged the knickers and lowered them inch by inch. When they were at her knees he let go and they fell to her ankles. Cathy lifted first one foot then the other and then she was free of everything that she had been wearing.

Nigel didn't touch her at first. He knew that was what she wanted but he also knew that the delay would increase her desire.

The first thing he did was blow a gentle stream of air. It was so gentle that her pubic hair barely moved, but it had the right affect. She moaned her appreciation.

He took a finger and ran it along the outside of her crack. Back and forth, back and forth, each time going a tiny bit deeper until eventually he broke through. She shuffled her feet until her legs were slightly apart. He pushed his finger into her hole and heard the satisfying squelch of her juices.

He removed his finger and looked at it. Slowly and deliberately he put it into his mouth. 'Tasty,' he said with a smile.

She smiled back, a faraway look in her eyes.

'Down,' he said patting the blanket. Obediently, Cathy bent her knees and crouched. She paused with her face close to his but Nigel ordered her down with his eyes. And she obeyed with a barely hidden smile.

She lay on her back with her legs bent at the knees. Her arms were stretched high above her head.

Nigel knelt at her feet. He ran his hands up her thighs until they rested on her knees. It took minimal force to prise them apart and she opened to him.

She murmured with delight when he flicked his tongue over her clitoris.

Having tasted enough of the sweetness he sat up. He put two fingers of his right hand inside her and started a gentle in and out rhythm. He used the fingers of his left hand to stimulate her.

'Fuck me,' she begged.

He ignored her pleadings and maintained his action until he sensed that she was ripe.

Once he was sure, he removed his hands and, taking hold of her hips, he moved himself into position and entered her.

Moaning with delight, she wrapped her legs around his back and they settled into a rhythm, their mutual pleasure increasing with each thrust.

Nigel congratulated himself. He had judged Cathy's ripeness to perfection and her orgasm exploded just seconds before his own.

Spent yet satisfied they lay awhile to catch their breath.

'Can I bring a friend next time?' Cathy asked.

He lifted himself onto his elbow and looked down at her, hardly able to believe his luck.

'My friend Margaret is looking for a driving instructor. You could teach us both.'

Much Ado (About Nothing)
by Sue Williams

I am not accustomed to seducing students, particularly when I'm lecturing on the bard. But there she was with her legs crossed – front row, notebook spread – and I admit my gaze fell and there you have it. I could say it was the approach of the twenty-fifth, or the snow that makes Cambridgeans hanker for warmth, but in fairness, I suppose I'd be lying. It was flesh and eyes – no, mostly flesh – and maybe a smattering of bard.

The lecture was about sex. Be not alarmed, dear reader. When one has studied literature for thirty years, one begins to get coitus on the brain. I usually say the bard is the worst, though, in fairness, it's Chaucer who *priketh harde and depe* and I have to admit there's more to dear Jane than meets the eye. (Had you ever wondered what went on beyond the haha? Be wary of coyness. It ruts beneath the silks.) This was what I sought to impart on the Friday morning in question, ostensibly to a dozen students, though I was actually addressing Ms Carson's thighs. These sported nylons and a skirt that played a purpose quite different to coverage or warmth. 'In fact,' I explained, as she uncrossed her legs, her knees a mere pinch apart, 'the 'Ado' in *Much Ado About Nothing*, might well have referred to sex. Evidence also suggests,' I went on, 'that to an Elizabethan, a 'thing' was, euphemistically, a phallus. This said, I put it to you that a *nothing* (or a 'no thing', if you will,) might well have represented the vagina. So there we have it. Freudian I admit. *A Lot of Sex Around A Vagina.*'

There was the usual ripple of mirth. Ms Carson, whose scarlet pout had steadily slouched, flashed me a filthy glare and re-crossed her legs. Thus came the thing that snatched me away – a flash, I fancied, of gusset. A wisp of lace as thin as her sheers (light, virginal and clearly rude) and I have always been so swayed by stocking tops – that gasp of flesh and strap. My own muscles stirred behind the lectern. I imagined her, sprawled in that very seat, moist beneath the lace; the crease where the thigh meets the slope of the sex as warm as a full-mouthed kiss. (The Medieval *prick* is so apt, don't you think? Hardness, if you'll pardon, can be needling.) I noticed, as I strained to return to my speech, that while the others took notes, Ms Carson did not. And as I watched, I grew more certain that all twelve of them, in their analytical fervour, had glimpsed my fixation. They saw and they flinched, with their taut flesh and hormones. And yet, with an idle stroke of her bosom, Ms Carson won me back.

I ask you, would you have sent her away? Milk-white skin, a swell of cashmere, black eyes coaled and filled with heat. No, no. She was a Desdemon. (And I had not made the beast with two backs since the Yuletide of '98.)

I asked her to stay behind. And so it was. I feigned authority, with a shuffle of papers, and Ms Carson waited and watched. I was aware, in my state of Adonisian excitement that the chance of this creature truly aching for me was, quite frankly, slim. And yet, I still wondered how she'd propose such an act: 'You gave me an F, now I'll return the favour'? 'Allow me to show you my *no thing*'? Or was I required to make the first move? If so, the price of failure could be steep.

Naturally, she did none of these things. As I reached up and cleaned the board, I heard her steps behind me. She climbed the platform and walked so close that I could smell the peppermint on her breath. I turned round. She was leaning against the table, which stood to the left of the lectern. The look in her eyes was especially louche. 'I noticed,' I said, walking up close, 'that you weren't taking notes.'

She shrugged and parted her knees. 'You're disgusting,' she said.

The heart in me fell.

'I mean it,' she went on. 'You, lecturing on sex like that: it's vile.'

'Ah,' I said. I coughed, once, into my fist. 'Well, Ms Carson, such is the nature of Shakespeare.'

'Touch me,' she said. As if to highlight where, she parted her knees a little more and stared at me with a filthy dilation.

'Ah,' I said, glancing down. 'I see.'

As I stood on this delicate moral precipice, there was but one thing that tipped me over the edge. The female form – beautiful as it is – arguably reaches its prime when the spine is bent back like a harp, and the curves, if you will – reach out to be plucked. Ms Carson now moulded herself in this way. Her lashes lowered, her thighs parted. She smelt more of musk than mint. With a free hand she grabbed mine, jerked me against her (I fear I fell clumsily) and thrust my fingers upwards. (Upwards to where, I shall not say. I am aware, dear reader, of the limits of taste.) I circled rather ineptly, charmed by her wetness, which grew behind the lace like an oyster from the swell. She let

207

out a sigh and tossed back her head, and this inspired my freer hand to reach down and unzip.

Mea culpa! In her palm, I was a sapling! And how roughly – but how faithfully! – she tore me from the earth! She gripped me firm, slipping free each pearlised button, until before me lay a bosom that could launch a thousand ships! How I, aged dolt, thrust myself within her, and cried between her thighs and poured confessions from my depths! Dear friend, I was transformed! I shuddered, quite Olympian! Her fountain washed me pure and I did drink!

The world, I fear, was spinning. I collapsed, against her neck. I thought I could hear her moaning, 'Again, again…'

'I'm sorry, my dear,' I murmured. 'I'm afraid I'm quite spent.'

She pushed me away, and I stumbled. She gave me the look of Iago. 'Give me an A!' she said, through her teeth. She sighed and rolled her eyes. 'I want you to give me an A!' Exhausted by the prospect of further carnality, I considered what an 'A' might be; but her face, alas, gave away her intention, and I saw that she was speaking of grades.

'Forgive me, my dear,' I shielded my manhood. 'But top grades are hardly likely, unless you make some notes.'

She rolled her eyes, and began to chew. 'Do I have to spell it out?' she said, grabbing me by the haunches. 'Give me an A for my essay, and I might forget to tell the Dean about your…' She glanced down at my tender parts, and added, 'Shall we say, *movements*.' Dear reader, I was shocked. Such indecency! Such filth! The serpent's tooth itself is not so thankless or so harsh!

'Indeed,' I said, regaining my pride, as I zipped myself secure. 'Should you *truly* merit an A, I would give you nothing less!'

She slipped from the desk, with succubae eyes. 'Well I do,' she said, with a toss of her head. 'I merit an A, and you know it.' And I watched her stride from the room, her hips swaying ahead of the rest, alarmed at the thought of my Faust-like demise.

She did not attend my lectures again, though I often pictured her sitting there, triumphant, thighs akimbo. But now, I fear I've misrepresented her. What can be said of that? Believe me, she *was* a Desdemon. Perhaps I'll rewrite her in iambs. And in her way, she saved me, for her essay *truly* deserved an A. My friend, it was exquisite! Believe me, for why should I lie? She wrote of misprision with the quickest of wits (and I fancied her pages smelt almost erogenous).

Also available from Xcite Books:
(www.xcitebooks.com)

Publication 14th February 2007

Sex & Seduction	**1905170785**	**price £7.99**
Sex & Satisfaction	**1905170777**	**price £7.99**
Sex & Submission	**1905170793**	**price £7.99**

Publication 14th May 2007

5 Minute Fantasies 1	**1905170610**	**price £7.99**
5 Minute Fantasies 2	**190517070X**	**price £7.99**
5 Minute Fantasies 3	**1905170718**	**price £7.99**

Publication 13th August 2007

Whip Me	**1905170920**	**price £7.99**
Spank Me	**1905170939**	**price £7.99**
Tie Me Up	**1905170947**	**price £7.99**

Publication 12th November 2007

Ultimate Sins	**1905170599**	**price £7.99**
Ultimate Sex	**1905170955**	**price £7.99**
Ultimate Submission	**1905170963**	**price £7.99**

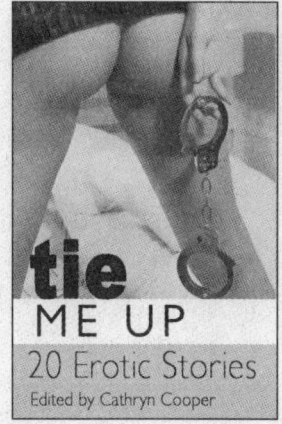

Whip Me	1905170920	price £7.99
Spank Me	1905170939	price £7.99
Tie Me Up	1905170947	price £7.99